# BOOK 2

# CAMP CANNIBAL

## Clay McLeod Chapman

Disney • Hyperion Books

New York

Printed in the United States of America
First Edition
1 3 5 7 9 10 8 6 4 2
G475-5664-5-14032

Library of Congress Cataloging-in-Publication Data
Chapman, Clay McLeod.
  Camp Cannibal / Clay McLeod Chapman.—First edition.
      pages cm.—(The tribe ; [2])
  Summary: Spencer Pendleton wants to make a fresh start when his father sends him
to Camp New Leaf but the Tribe is there, planning to put down roots, and Spencer
must stop them before someone is seriously hurt—or worse.
  ISBN 978-1-4231-5222-4 (hardback)
  [1. Secret societies—Fiction. 2. Conduct of life—Fiction. 3. Camps—Fiction.
4. Missing children—Fiction.] I. Title.
  PZ7.C366373Cam 2014
  [Fic]—dc23          2013051273

Reinforced binding

Visit www.DisneyBooks.com

SUSTAINABLE FORESTRY INITIATIVE    Certified Sourcing
www.sfiprogram.org
SFI-00993

THIS LABEL APPLIES TO TEXT STOCK

for Jasper

Dear Dad . . .

If you're reading this, that can only mean one thing:

A. I'm dead and buried somewhere in the woods surrounding Camp New Leaf, my body now a buffet for maggots.

B. I've been arrested and am serving a life sentence for crimes I didn't commit.

C. Me (and my lungs) are on the run.

You sold me out. If you'd been paying attention, you would've realized I'm as good as ghosted by now. How could you do this to me? Your own son? You might as well have hand-delivered me to the Tribe wrapped up in a bow. . . .

I wish I could tell you face-to-face the things that you're about to read. Man to man. Isn't that what this summer was supposed to be about in the first place? "Manning" up? Those were the last words you said before forcing me to board the bus that brought me to this maximum-security teen penal colony.

Man.

Up.

If I make it out alive, I'll have a lot of explaining to do. If I don't, hopefully someone will find this notebook, see your name and address, and deliver it to you. Then maybe one day you'll understand why I did what I had to do. Maybe.

But let's get this out of the way up front: I did not overthrow my summer camp.

Honest.

Here. I'll prove it to you. . . .

Your son,
Spencer

# Part 1: Fight the Fog

*One has a moral responsibility to disobey unjust laws. I would agree with St. Augustine that "an unjust law is no law at all."*
—Martin Luther King Jr.

# IMAGINARY FRIENDS

There never was any Tribe.

No Peashooter. No Sporkboy. No Compass. No Yardstick. No Sully.

Turns out that taking the fall for a cult of "teenage headhunters" allegedly living within the walls of my middle school had some very real, very severe legal ramifications for me. After the whole cafeteria contamination episode, not only was I expelled from Greenfield Middle, but I had to stand in front of a judge and swear I would never lace another lunchroom's cranberry sauce with a highly psychoactive basidiomycete fungus ever again.

Fair enough.

Because I threw myself on the mercy of the court, the dishonorable judge sentenced me to . . .

House arrest.

Mom had already condemned me to live with my father. Not that I blamed her. After the earthquake I'd put her through, she couldn't deal anymore.

Lights dim. Spotlight on Dad's grand entrance back into my life.

"What did I miss?" he asked like this was all some kind of sitcom. Cue canned laugh track, followed by uproarious applause from audience.

*Dad to the rescue.*

Must've fit me into his hectic work schedule. Whenever his presence is required for some impromptu parenting, he's always a no-show, thanks to some last-minute business-related thingy popping up.

Or was he on vacation with his new *girlfiend*?

The excuses blur together after a while.

My dad usually times his appearances to whenever a principal or a judge is around to notice. Then he's the hero swooping in to save the day—while mom is left looking like *The Bad Mother, The Unfit Parent, The Careless Custodian.*

Not anymore. Not as of December.

Now it was Dad's turn to look after me.

*Heaven help us all.*

All I ever get is the parental shell. Mannequin dad. I could create a line of My Very Own Dad dolls, complete with three prerecorded automated responses:

*"Sure thing!"*

*"What's that?"*

*"Okeydoke!"*

As in—"Dad, do you mind if I bust out of the house for a bit? Cabin fever's kicking in big-time and I need a break."

*"Sure thing!"*

"Did you hear what I just said, Dad?"

*"What's that?"*

"Never mind."

*"Okeydoke!"*

*Additional responses sold separately.*

But house arrest has a few perks. Like the lovely little fashion accessory shackled to my ankle for the last six months—a box bejeweled with a flashing red light and a hundred feet of freedom.

Not an inch more.

If I were to step off of Dad's property, even for a second, the proximity sensor latched to my ankle would rat me out.

I had a total of thirty seconds to return to the cozy confines of my hundred feet of freedom—or else, at exactly thirty-one seconds, it would send a distress signal to mission control and a patrol car would be dispatched to hunt me down.

I was a jailbird sentenced to six months of homeschooled purgatory.

No television.

No Internet.

No cell.

Nothing but time to, as the judge put it, "reflect" on all of my "appalling transgressions" and learn how to be "a more upstanding citizen."

I used those empty hours to bone up on the Tribal Required Reading List:

*Lord of the Flies*, by William Golding.

*White Fang*, by Jack London.

*The Call of the Wild*, by London, too.

*The Outsiders*, by S. E. Hinton.

*Watership Down*, by Richard Adams.

*The Adventures of Tom Sawyer*, by Mark Twain.

*The Art of War*, by Sun Tzu.

*Johnny Tremain*, by Esther Forbes.

*The Red Badge of Courage*, by Stephen Crane.

Every book that my ol' pal Peashooter had cribbed from over the years.

Why read them now?

If I read in between the lines, read deeper, I hoped that I'd come upon some clue as to where the Tribe ran off to.

So far, nothing.

• • •

One hour out of every week, I was granted access to the world beyond my ankle bracelet for a visit with Dr. Vladimir Lobotov.

During our first session, my fuzzy-eyebrowed psychiatrist

pulled out a stack of note cards. Splattered across each was a different inkblot, like a fountain pen had blown its nose—if, you know, fountain pens had noses.

"What do you see here?" Dr. Lobotomy asked as he held up a card.

It looked like a butterfly.

"Let's see," I started. "I do believe I'm looking at a boy, somewhere around the age of fifteen to seventeen, who seems to be gripping a pair of plastic protractors from geometry class in each of his fists. It would appear that the protractors have been lined with . . . Are those X-ACTO blades? I do believe so."

Dr. Lobotomy flipped the card over to study it himself. His left caterpillar arched on his forehead. "You see all of that . . . ?"

"Of course," I said. "Why? What do *you* see, Doc?"

When it comes to messing with authority figures, I really can't help myself.

It's a problem I have.

Lobotomy flashed another card at me. "What about this one?"

I saw a rabbit with long ears.

"This one's a cinch," I said. "I see a girl. Pretty cute, but don't tell her I told you that. Her freckled face is half-hidden behind her endless auburn hair. She's wearing a gym uniform lined with an exoskeleton of—wait, let me see—yes, *yes*, I do believe those are safety pins. She seems to be gripping a slingshot, aimed right at me. I wouldn't mess with her, if I were you. She's quite the sharpshooter. Just out of curiosity, Doc—have you seen anyone fitting that description around here lately?"

That performance quickly earned me a prescription for Chlorofornil.

I can hear the commercial jingle ringing through my skull now . . .

*When you're about to cross the border*
*Into that rocky mood disorder*
*Just pop this lovely lil' pill*
*We like to call Chlorofornil!*

*Yes—Chlorofornil! The cure-all for freedom of the mind! Just pop a lovely little tablet before every meal and say bon voyage to independent thought forever! Your neurotransmitters will be restored to their docile levels once again, as good as cattle!*

*Say good-bye to depression*
*Or any emotional regression*
*All it takes is one lil' pill*
*So swallow some Chlorofornil!\**

---

*\*Use only as directed. Possible side effects may include confusion, blurry vision, dry mouth, nausea, constipation, headaches, muscle aches, anxiety, insomnia, restlessness. Even nightmares. Lots and lots of nightmares. Tell your doctor if you have any pre-existing medical conditions before taking Chlorofornil. Contact your physician if you experience any of the following: A strong sense of eyes always on you, an overwhelming feeling of constant surveillance from an invisible but palpable presence, an impending sense of doom, that trouble is on the horizon, that your imaginary friends want to kill you, that you are not alone even when you are alone, that there is a tribe of runaway teenagers somewhere out there in this world who probably want to string you up by your feet and play piñata with your body right about now. Talk to your health-care professional to see if Chlorofornil is right for you!*

This antidepressant was supposed to treat my newly diagnosed mood disorder—but for every symptom your meds fix, you suddenly have ten additional side effects to wrestle with. My personal favorite:

*Halluuuuuucinations.*

There are times when I'll be reading a book and the letters will start wriggling away across the page without me, like a swarm of ants.

How's that for *better living through chemistry?*

My mind really isn't what it used to be.

Sometimes the phone will ring and I'll pick it up, only to be greeted by dead air. Sounds like there's a ghost on the other end of the line.

"Hello . . . ?"

Silence. I swear I can hear somebody breathing into the receiver—but whoever that phantasmal prank caller is, they won't say a word to me.

"Sully . . . ? That you?"

*Click.* Dial tone.

But just as long as I'm not make-believing my imaginary friends are trying to kill me, everything is peachy keen as far as my headshrinker is concerned.

Dr. Lobotomy pontificated that I had conjured up this "band of runaway kids" as "a coping mechanism" for my own "aberrant behavior."

Whatever that means.

"They are figments of a rather highly active imagination," he told my dad. "Nothing but the product of your son's excitable mind."

But you want to know the craziest part?

I was beginning to forget their faces.

Except for Sully.

I still had her missing flyer. It felt like cheating, but I had to peek at it to remind myself what she looked like.

At night, I'd close my eyes and try focusing all my thoughts on her features, as if I was cramming for some exam.

I'd try remembering the color of her eyes.

The slope of her nose.

The curve of her lips when she smiled.

*Whatever you do, Spencer,* I'd say to myself, *you can't forget her. Just hold on to her.*

*Hold on.*

*Hold . . .*

The chemical fog of Chlorofornil would roll over my cerebrum, thick as Peashooter soup. Sully's features became faint, and before long I couldn't see her at all through the murky miasma clouding my memory.

*Fight the fog, Spencer. Fight it.*

Too late. She was gone again.

I'd open my eyes and find her staring back at me from her flyer. She almost looked disappointed.

"I'm sorry, Sully. . . ."

As a part of Dr. Lobotomy's therapeutic plan for me, I keep a daily diary. I now have to take this journal with me wherever I go and scribble down my feelings. If I don't feel like talking to my dad or if I don't think anybody would believe me—I write about it here.

A journal doesn't judge. A journal doesn't care if I'm crazy or not.

So I've decided to use these pages to help me remember.

I can jot down whatever recollections of the Tribe I have left before the fog sweeps in and tries to take them away.

*Maybe I'll try sketching a portrait of Peashooter. . . .*

*Maybe I'll write a historical account of the Tribe's exploits at Greenfield. . . .*

*Maybe I'll tell Sully all the things I wish I could have said to her in person when I had the chance, but never did. . . .*

*Maybe . . .*

Maybe I am crazy.

# THE MAILBOXES ARE WHISPERING AGAIN

April thirteenth.

*Happy birthday, Spence . . . You survived another year.*

Barely.

Fourteen whopping years old.

Sure doesn't seem like Dad remembered. The day is still young, but I'm not holding my breath on any surprise parties popping up.

Some emergency business thingy has had him on the phone all afternoon. Or was it his girlfiend again? He swore up and down that it'd only be a few minutes.

That was an hour ago.

I was just about to knock on his office door, but my knuckles halted when I heard his voice. Pressing my ear against the paneling, I listened to his half of the conversation—"You think he'd be happy there? I need all the help I can get. Send me a pamphlet."

I walked in. Dad looked at me and held up a finger, as if to say—*Just one more minute*. I suddenly felt the compulsion to chomp his pointer off. Whoever was on the other line was still talking, forcing Dad to choose which of us to listen to.

Guess who won that battle?

"Dad," I said. "I was thinking about taking the car out for a little spin."

*"Sure thing."*

"Where did you leave the keys?"

*"What's that?"*

"Don't worry, I'll find them. . . ."

*"Okeydoke!"*

• • •

Wandering about the perimeters of our property line, I decided to test my ankle monitor. Make sure it was still up to snuff.

*Just dip a toe into the great wild beyond our grass and see if . . .*

The second I planted my foot into the street, the red light on my ankle bracelet started to flicker. The countdown to Big Brother barging in began:

*Thirty . . .*

*Twenty-nine . . .*

*Twenty-eight . . .*

*Twenty-seven . . .*

*Twenty-six . . .*

I dragged my foot back onto the lawn. The bloody pulse steadied itself again.

Seems to be working just fine, I thought.

*Psst, kid,* somebody whispered behind my back. *Over here.*

I turned to find our mailbox staring at me from its post. Its aluminum lid curled back like a silver lip and smiled.

*Happy birthday,* it said.

I took a step back.

I really needed to talk to Lobotomy about adjusting my prescription.

*I got something for you, birthday boy. . . .*

I was not about to have a conversation with my mailbox.

*Come on,* it said. *Just reach in, kid. I'm not gonna bite. . . .*

I'd never stuffed my hand down the gullet of a talking mailbox before. Just as I was about to reach in, the lid snapped at my fingers.

*Sorry about that.* The mailbox chortled. *Couldn't help myself.*

"It's okay," I said, reaching in. "I'd probably do the same thing."

There was a package waiting for me inside.

Nobody ever sends me mail.

There was no return address on the manila envelope. Just a dozen mismatched stamps stuck to the front. I greedily tore it open and pulled out . . .

*A book?*

It was a well-worn copy of J. M. Barrie's *Peter Pan.* There was no note, no inscription inside. Just a ratty paperback that must've been read a hundred times.

But who sent it?

*You know who*, the mailbox said, reading my thoughts.

Flipping through, I came upon a single underlined sentence:

*Never say good-bye because saying good-bye means going away and going away means forgetting.*

I quickly closed the book and scanned our block.

"This is a practical joke, isn't it?" I asked. "You're messing with my head."

No response. *Of course.* What did I think it would say?

It's just a mailbox.

There's only one person I know who knows I know they've read *Peter Pan*. And that certain person just might know that I'd know that they'd know I knew.

This was the best birthday present a guy could get.

*Hope.*

# THE GREAT ESCAPES

lame Martin Luther King.

Mom had to arrange my homeschooling when she realized Dad had forgotten to. I still had a semester's worth of seventh grade to survive, and she wasn't about to let me slip through the academic cracks. That meant tackling the Age of Enlightenment, square roots, and sentence structure all on my own—not to mention a whole bunch of other subjects that blurred into a chemically induced stew of misplaced integers and grammatical mistakes.

You try studying on this prescription. Class might as well have been underwater. There was a thickness to my thoughts after I popped one of these pills, slowing my synapses down. My brain had to push through sludge to reach the answers.

*Fight the fog fight the fog fight the fog fight the fog . . .*

But then I met Dr. King.

He was waiting for me in my history lesson. I read about how he fought for his beliefs in a nonviolent manner.

"You're telling me you stood up against injustice peacefully?" I asked. "Protest with a smile? That sort of thing?"

*"Nonviolence is a powerful and just weapon,"* he answered back from the cozy confines of my history book. *"Indeed, it is a weapon unique in history, which cuts without wounding and ennobles the man who wields it."*

This is what happens when I study.

My books start talking back to me.

All Dad had to do was make sure I kept up with my class assignments. That usually amounted to him peeking his head into my room for a quick scan. As long as he saw a book in my hands, open and right-side up, he didn't look much further.

One night, he poked his head into my room for a quick look-see. Just as he was about to slip back out, I felt compelled to ask him—"Did you know Martin Luther King once said, *'A man who won't die for something is not fit to live'?*"

*"Sure thing."*

"So what are you willing to die for, Dad?"

*"What's that?"*

"Nothing. Just thinking out loud."

*"Okeydoke!"*

He closed the door behind him, sealing me in with Martin. I wanted to make my room even smaller, encasing myself within my history book. Let the pages become my walls.

What was I willing to die for?

How about *who*?

I'll give you one guess.

• • •

Fifteen breakouts in the last three months alone.

Not a bad personal record, huh? When you're under house arrest, you have to find ways to stretch the ol' legs.

Of course I'd get caught. I never tampered with my ankle monitor. I kept it on, leading the police right to me.

Here are my top three breakouts of all time.

So far.

# GREAT ESCAPE HALL OF FAME
## ESCAPE #3: APRIL TWENTIETH
### THE LOCAL LIBRARY

I had some overdue books, so I decided to hand-deliver them.

All I had was a thirty-second head start. Thirty seconds before my ankle monitor would break out into a hissy fit.

Let's break this down:

• If I ran fast enough, I could reach the end of the block in thirteen seconds.

- The next block in twenty-eight.
- The local branch of our public library was five blocks away.
- I'd have three blocks to go by the time the cops knew I was officially off the reservation.
- If we estimate that each block takes roughly twelve seconds to span, that planted me at the library's front entrance thirty-three seconds after my ankle monitor tipped Big Brother off to my whereabouts.
- Standard police response time: Two minutes, twenty-seven seconds.

My math was feeling a little fuzzy, but if my calculations were correct—I would have somewhere between one minute and fifty-seven seconds to two minutes all to myself before the authorities rolled in and dragged me away.

A bookworm can do a lot of damage with two minutes in the library.

Why not take the opportunity to peruse the newspaper archives on the Internet for sightings of feral teenagers?

Anything that might help me figure out where the Tribe had run off to.

Sully had to be out there, somewhere.

I just had to find her.

I kneeled down next to the mailbox at the edge of our yard, assuming my best sprint starting position.

Remember My Little Friend? You'd hardly even recognize

my inhaler anymore. I've "pimped my ride" since you last saw him. He now has red-and-yellow flames wrapping around the mouthpiece.

I brought him up to my lips and pumped my chest full of medicated air. Feeling my bronchioles embrace the aerosolized dose of corticosteroids, I waited for the starting pistol to fire off in my imagination and make a break for it.

*On your mark . . .*

*Get set . . .*

*Go!*

I'd like to go on record stating that I personally have nothing against the Greenfield County Police Department or any of its employees, particularly Officers Winston Sellars and James Cassidy. These gentlemen were only doing their job, and I have nothing but the utmost respect for them and their tireless work ethic. I wholeheartedly apologize for repeatedly putting them in the position of breaking a sweat.

*You know I love you guys . . . Right?*

Sellars was a squat, pug-faced patrolman, whose head barely reached his partner's shoulder. The handles on his horseshoe mustache got lost somewhere within the creases of his double chin.

Cassidy had more height and less weight. His gangly limbs left him looking like the dancing windsock you'd find outside a used-car dealership.

As soon as I saw them stumble into the library, a bit winded from their run, I flashed them a grin.

"Officers! I didn't know you had a membership to this branch. We should start our own book group."

"Time to go, Pendleton," Sellars said. "Put the book down slowly, *slowly.*"

"Don't you two ever get tired of the roles society has assigned us?" I asked. "I mean, you're both Authority figures with a capital *A*. I get that. You've got this part to play, just like I do. You look at me and all you see is a Delinquent with a capital *D*, a natural born absconder—and in all fairness, I was born for the role. But don't you think maybe, *just maybe*, we can put down these clichéd designations that destiny has doomed us to fulfill and see each other not for our differences, but for our commonalities? Can't we, you know . . . just get along?"

Sellars side-glanced Cassidy.

Cassidy cleared his throat. "Let's try not to make a scene, okay?"

"Of course," I complied. "But before we go, can I recommend some reading material for your next stakeout? I just finished this book that I think you two'll love."

"What book?" Sellars asked. Cassidy elbowed him in the ribs.

"It's called *I Know Why the Caged Jailbird's Ankle Monitor Sings*," I said. "I think it's somewhere in the romance section."

Thinking quick, I tipped over a stack of romance novels waiting to be reshelved and booked it down the aisle. Sellars planted his foot on a bodice ripper, slipping on the paperback like it was a banana peel.

Cassidy was right behind me. I jumped up onto the reference

desk, leaping over a few readers' heads as I scurried across the tabletop.

Undeterred, Cassidy grabbed at my knees. I avoided his clasping hands by hopping onto the next table, making sure not to step on anybody's reading material, like some kind of clumsy ballerina dancing *en pointe*.

Cassidy sped to the end of the table, cutting me off, and I froze with one foot still hovering through the air.

Perfect arabesque.

"Get down from there, Pendleton. *Now.*"

Cassidy was coming up fast. No more tables for me to scale.

The bookshelf just next to me suddenly looked a lot like a ladder.

So I started climbing.

Sellars picked himself up and followed Cassidy through the rows just below me—two mice maneuvering about a maze—as I leapt from one bookcase to the next.

"You are not lab rats," I belted out with each leap. "There is no cheese waiting at the end of this labyrinth! You're all free! Free to think for yourselves! Free to live your lives the way you want to! Freedom! *Freeeeeeedom!*"

I was running out of bookshelves. Only one more to go before I hit the wall.

But I was going for the gold here.

Or a window. Whichever came first.

I launched off the shelf with enough force to inadvertently

send the bookcase beneath me tipping over in the opposite direction.

I went one way, the shelf went another.

Once I landed on the last bookcase, I quickly spun around to behold the horrifying sight of the ledge I'd just left toppling into the neighboring case.

And the next.

Books slid off their shelves, their covers flapping haplessly through the air like flightless chickens falling to the floor as the chain reaction gained momentum.

All I could do was watch in shock as each shelf collided with the case beside it, one after another, sending patrons and police officers clearing the aisles.

I had unintentionally invented a new sporting event:

Library dominoes.

# GREAT ESCAPE HALL OF FAME
## ESCAPE #2: APRIL THIRTIETH
### GREENFIELD MIDDLE SCHOOL

Is it my fault Doc Lobotomy never asked *which* bathroom I planned on using?

So what if I'd picked one from my old alma mater?

I knew it was a big no-no, coming back to Greenfield Middle—but I needed to see someone.

Mr. Simms's face blanched as soon as he opened the janitor's closet and discovered me inside, waiting among the shelves of cleaning fluids.

"Good lord, son," he said. "How long have you been in here?"

I knew my police escorts were on their way, so I didn't waste any time with chitchat. "Have you heard from them?"

"Who?"

Nobody knew Mr. Simms had been the Tribe's elder statesman but me. I had kept his secret, which meant he kept his job.

"You know who."

Simms scanned the hall to make sure we were alone.

"They could be anywhere by now," he said, shaking his head. "Hopefully far away from here."

"But they must've told you *something*."

"I told them not to."

"Why?"

"Because I knew you'd come for me and try to find out."

I couldn't help but wince. "You're protecting them *from me*?"

Mr. Simms reached into his pocket. "I did get this. . . ."

A postcard.

There was nothing written on the back, save for the school's address, care of Mr. Simms. It could have been from anybody.

But I knew who. "It's Sully, isn't it?"

"Your guess is as good as mine," Simms shrugged.

I flipped it over and found a faded photograph of a lake on the front. A crew-cutted kid straight out of the nineteen sixties was squatting in a canoe, waving at the camera.

At the top, it read:

## GREETINGS FROM LAKE WENDIGO!

Sellars and Cassidy stepped up behind Simms, looking none too happy.

"Officers!" I beamed, stuffing the postcard into my back pocket. "So glad you could make it."

"You gonna come peacefully this time," Cassidy asked, "or are we gonna have to use handcuffs?"

"Don't you two ever get tired of this routine? Don't you ever imagine there's more to life than this cat-and-mousing we find ourselves locked in, day after day?"

"Not again, kid," Sellars sighed. "Either do as we tell you, or we use force."

"I love it when you go all authoritarian, Officer Sellars. . . ."

"Count of three, Pendleton," Cassidy intoned. *"One."*

I turned to Mr. Simms. "What period are we in?"

"Third."

*"Two."*

"That means you just mopped the halls in the cafeteria, didn't you?"

"Just finished," he said.

"Right on schedule." I nodded. "Good to see you, Mr. Simms."

*"Three."*

I plowed past Sellars and Cassidy.

"Come back here!" Cassidy shouted.

"But you haven't gotten a tour of the school yet," I called over my shoulder. "Follow me!"

Sellars and Cassidy were on my heels. Sellars was slowing down but Cassidy kept right on me.

"If you're feeling peckish," I called, entering the cafeteria, "might I recommend the mashed potatoes and a dash of pepper spray. Simply divine!"

The floor shone like a fresh ice-skating rink. If I had the time to stop, I could have marveled at my own reflection.

Cassidy was only a few steps behind. Just when he reached out to grab my shoulder, I dropped into a perfect slider. By the time Cassidy caught on, he was already heading on a crash course for the hot-food steam tables.

"Whoa, whoa, whoa—" Cassidy skidded his heels into the linoleum, only to slip. Arms flailing, he tried to correct his balance as best he could, flinging one foot into the air as if he were a lumbering figure skater performing a camel spin.

Cassidy made impact with the steam table—*THWACK*—sending a hailstorm of chicken nuggets into the air and showering back down upon him.

"Whenever you're ready for round two, just let me know," I said, picking up a nugget and taking a bite. "No rush. Take your time. Rest a sec."

Cassidy rolled over the floor, covered in nuggets, moaning low.

I held out my inhaler to him. "Here. Let me freshen you up."

Sellars ran into the cafeteria, hyperventilating, blocking my exit.

So this was where I'd take my last stand.

*Showdown at the OK Cafeteria.*

I clambered behind the steam tables, quickly presented with a vast array of dining choices.

*What do we have on the menu today?*

From the looks of it, we had a wide selection of foods to choose from—green peas and cubed carrots, baked beans with bacon bits drifting in bubbling brown sauce, a washed-out fruit salad, mac n' cheese, along with our aforementioned arsenal of chicken nuggets—each sitting in its own stainless steel heating tray.

A plastic-handled serving scoop pierced the surface of each grub tub.

I grabbed for the nearest ladle and served Sellars a hearty dollop of baked beans, splattered across the front of his uniform.

I seized a second scoop, double-fisting now, brandishing both like a pair of six shooters.

"Make sure you get a bit of all four food groups," I shouted as I fired off a scoop of mac n' cheese with my left hand, and peas with my right.

I'd become a culinary quick-draw.

Cassidy clamored up from the floor just in time to receive a face full of fruit salad. I was rapid-firing now, ladling up and hurling away.

"Eat melon balls, coppers!"

Both officers shielded their faces and stormed the steam tables.

That left the kitchen. I rushed into the back area, quickly met by a posse of hairnetted lunch ladies prepping for today's meal.

"Surprise health inspection!" I shouted before bolting for the storage freezer.

A bean-battered Sellars took the left while a mac-n'-cheesed Cassidy took the right, cornering me and closing in.

I tried sidestepping them, but they pounced before I could push through.

"I'm getting really tired of your routine, kid," Sellars said as he dragged me out of the kitchen, my heels squealing over the linoleum.

"That's what I've been saying all this time! But what else am I supposed to do with myself, locked up all day? The only way I can get you guys to come visit is when I break out from house arrest."

"Try and get some friends your own age."

Mr. Simms had entered the cafeteria, wheeling in his mop and bucket.

"My friends broke out a long time ago," I said. "I'm trying to find them."

"If you do, tell them I said hello," Simms said.

I could tell he missed them.

He wasn't the only one.

# GREAT ESCAPE HALL OF FAME
## ESCAPE #1: MAY TWENTIETH
### THE TULLIVER RESIDENCE

I've had to time my breakouts between my med intake. It's easier to escape on a clear head.

Dinner wasn't for another hour. The fog was only one pill away—but for now, my mind felt free and clear. Nothing but blue skies in my brain.

Perfect for a little evening run.

"I think I'm gonna go for a stroll around the block, Dad," I called upstairs.

*"Sure thing,"* Dad shouted back from his office.

"Don't wait up."

*"What's that?"*

"Never mind."

*"Okeydoke!"*

There was no telling how long I had before the SWAT team would swoop in, so I had to be quick. There were several miles between me and my destination.

Luckily, I remembered the way, and the dark offered me enough cover to run without raising any suspicion. I just had to avoid streets with heavy traffic and any well-lit neighborhoods.

Once I made it to the front steps, I rang the bell and waited for the door to open.

And waited.

And waited.

"Come on, come on, come on . . ."

I pounded on the door.

Nobody answered.

The red light on my ankle monitor was flashing frantically. Any minute now it would draw the cops right to me.

I pressed my finger down on the bell again, holding it in place this time, the ring reverberating through the halls of the house just on the other side of the door.

"Answer the door, answer the door, answer—"

The door opened by just a crack. I saw nothing but black.

"Who is it?" a voice asked.

"Mr. Tulliver . . . ?"

The chain-lock stretched to its hilt, revealing a sliver of a man's heavily bearded face peering out from the dark confines of the hallway.

"What do you want?"

"You, uh—you probably don't remember me, but—"

"You're that boy," he interrupted. "Sully's friend."

Over my shoulder, I spotted the squad car slowly rolling down the block. The headlights reached across the street, searching for me.

*My time's running out.*

"Mind if I come inside? Maybe we could talk. . . ."

"You told me not to give up on her."

"Please, Mr. Tulliver. I need to know if she—"

"You said Sully wasn't dead," he interrupted. "That I shouldn't give up hope."

Gravel crumbled as the squad car pulled into Mr. Tulliver's driveway.

"Has she visited you?" I asked. "Have there been any . . . sightings of her?"

I heard the squad car doors open and slam shut, followed by footsteps.

"Mr. Pendleton," Cassidy said behind me. "We meet again."

I refused to look over my shoulder, focusing on Mr. Tulliver. "Have you seen her? Has she called? *Anything?* Please, sir . . ."

His face disappeared into the darkness of the house. "I found this pinned to the front door one morning. . . ."

Mr. Tulliver slipped a single piece of paper through the crack in the door.

It was a page torn out from a book. I read over it and quickly realized it was *Peter Pan*. At the very center of the page, there was a single sentence underlined:

> *Just always be waiting for me. . . .*

I felt the swell of hope rise up within my chest.

"Thank you, Mr. Tulliver," I said before handing it back

and turning to face my ever-patient escorts. "Evening, officers. Lovely night for a stroll, isn't it?"

"This ends tonight, Pendleton," Sellars said. "No more slaps on the wrist."

"Wouldn't have it any other way."

"Into the car," Cassidy said.

"Give me a head start?"

"No."

"Close your eyes and count to ten?"

"No."

"Your shoe's untied?"

"Sorry—no."

I bolted. One last time. Cassidy lunged for me, tripping on his shoelace. He toppled onto Sellars while I ducked around the side of the house.

My chest felt raw.

I tugged on my inhaler slung around my neck. With the help of My Little Friend, I picked up the pace and ran as fast as my lungs would allow.

The clear sky was pockmarked with stars, and the full moon was directly overhead.

I really should get out more.

Just for fun, for freedom, sweet freedom, I skidded to a halt in the middle of the street and howled—"*Ooooowoooooooooooooh!*"

That got the neighbors' attention. Porch lights were flashing on all along the block. Window curtains were pulled back to reveal the silhouettes of people inside.

I howled again, louder this time—"Ow-ow-*owoooooooooooh!*"

Even as the flashing blue and red lights from the squad car bathed my body, I continued to bay at the moon, recalling one of Peashooter's favorite quotes:

*"And when, on the still cold nights, he pointed his nose at a star and howled long and wolflike, it was his ancestors, dead and dust, pointing nose at star and howling down through the centuries and through him."*

*The Call of the Wild.*

I howled until my lungs were inflamed and sore from the cold night air—*"Ow-ow-owoooooooooooh!"*

• • •

Cassidy kept his hand clamped on my shoulder as we waited for Dad to answer the door.

When Dad did, he crossed his arms and leaned against the frame.

"Look who's back," he said. "Sure you don't want to keep him, officers?"

"Good to see you, too, Dad."

"Sir." Officer Sellars cleared his throat. "The court was pretty clear what would happen if this kind of behavior continued."

Dad took me by the arm and yanked me inside the house. "Don't worry, officers. I think I've found just the place for him. . . ."

*What happened to My Very Own Dad doll? This one's off script.*

I pulled out of his grip. "What's that supposed to mean?"

"I had a nice conversation with an old pal of yours from Greenfield. He told me all about this place just out of town where you can run your little heart out."

"*Friend?*" I asked. "I don't have any friends. Especially not at Greenfield."

"Don't give me that," he said. "That kind of act might've worked on your mother, but I'm not falling for it."

"Who was it? Was it a girl?"

"You're not talking your way out of this one." Dad grabbed my arm again. I pulled back, nearly falling into Sellars and Cassidy.

"I'm not playing these games all summer long. Your mother might've had the patience for it, but I'm not putting up with it."

"Stop acting like this is Mom's fault."

"Does that mean you're going to finally take some responsibility for your actions?"

"Why don't *you* take some responsibility? Just admit you don't know the first thing about me. Admit it!"

Cassidy cleared his throat. "Just keep a close eye on him, sir. We'll let you—"

"Go ahead," Dad kept barking. "Blame me. Somehow every mess you've gotten yourself into is my fault."

"How would you know?" I asked. "This is the most you've said to me in months. *Months!* Your parenting has been on autopilot since I got here."

Dad hesitated. His mouth opened, but the words weren't there.

I waited. So did Sellars and Cassidy, who had just snagged themselves ringside seats at our first family throw-down.

"You don't treat my house like a home," Dad finally mustered. "It's a rest stop to you. You're here long enough to use the bathroom, and then you're running away."

"It's your house," I said. "That doesn't mean it's my home."

"So—what? You'd rather stay with your mother?"

"*Yes!* A million times more!"

"That's too bad. She won't take you back. She'll never take you back now."

I flinched. Sellars, too.

"Want to know why?" Dad kept going, cutting and cutting and cutting. "Because you pushed her away. You pushed her until she got fed up with you."

I backed into Sellars and Cassidy.

"You did that, Spencer. Not me. Not your imaginary friends. Just you."

"Go to hell, Dad."

"I already got you a ticket," he said, putting an end to the conversation. "You're leaving in the morning."

• • •

The pamphlet was waiting for me on the kitchen counter. It must have arrived in the mail that afternoon. Was it too much to ask our mailbox to have chewed it up and spat it out before Dad could've read it?

I picked up the brochure and opened it. I couldn't believe what I was reading.

*This does not look good, Spencer. . . .*

# WELCOME TO CAMP NEW LEAF!

## AN ALTERNATIVE SUMMER CAMP EXPERIENCE FOR CHILDREN IN NEED OF SPECIALIZED CARE.

Camp New Leaf focuses on experiential therapy as a means of building self-esteem. We are a wilderness program, not a boot camp. New Leaf blends traditional camp activities with group therapy to help boys with behavioral problems face their own personal issues and grow in character.

Our campers include children with ADD/ADHD, learning disabilities, and emotional problems. Characteristics like lying, defiance, hostility, willfulness, oppositional attitude, and disobedience are all manageable behaviors that can be modified when given the opportunity to focus and meditate.

Cooperative team-building activities are at the core of our therapeutic process: hiking, canoeing, high ropes course, white-water rafting—as well as daily group sessions with fellow campers and trained counselors.

When everyone else has turned their backs on your children, let Camp New Leaf welcome them in with open arms!

# Part II: Turning Over a New Leaf

*He had been suddenly jerked from the heart of civilization*
*and flung into the heart of things primordial.*
—Jack London, *The Call of the Wild*

# TURNING OVER A NEW LEAF

I noticed the totem pole first. Six heads staring at me through my bus window.

*Talk about one heck of a welcoming committee. . . .*

Each hand-carved head grimaced under the weight of those above. The one at the very bottom stuck out a tongue from between gritted teeth, and its eyes seemed to follow our bus as we pulled into the parking lot. I would have said I saw it wink at me, but maybe that was just my medication playing tricks on me.

That totem pole might have an extra head by the time summer wrapped up.

Mine, if I wasn't careful.

*Just keep your head down, Spencer.*

I rubbed my ankle. No more monitor for me. Not out here in the middle of nowhere.

I hadn't said a word the entire bus ride. I had simply stared out the window and watched civilization disappear, one building at a time. The world had shifted from metal and glass to wood and grass in a matter of hours.

The bus lurched to a halt, and my head slammed into the back of the seat in front of me. The kid sitting there spun around, chewing on his fingernail. He had brown hair, a thick face, and a scab on his chin.

"Watch it," he said, spitting a sliver of his thumbnail. The crescent moon landed in my lap. His chapped lips peeled back to reveal braces.

"Sorry," I said and turned my attention out my window.

A banner hung between two trees directly outside. It had the image of a moose head—only instead of antlers, a pair of maple leaves branched out from its skull.

# TIME TO TURN OVER A NEW LEAF!

"Welcome to Camp New Leaf," our driver announced. "Now get out."

The retractable metal doors on our bus fanned open with a sigh and exhaled its adolescent passengers.

Humidity clung to my skin like a moist sponge.

I took in a deep breath of clean country air.

This place didn't seem so bad, I thought. Seems kinda nice, actually.

*Who knows? I might end up liking it here.*

Besides, it's hard to feel homesick when you don't have a home to feel sick about.

## SURVIVAL STRATEGY #3:
### LOCATE YOUR AUTHORITY FIGURES.

I spotted a balding man with a ponytail holding a clipboard.

For those keeping tabs, this was George Galloway, our camp director. A strip of zinc oxide ran down his nose. He wore cut-off shorts and a T-shirt with NEW LEAF ironed across the chest, along with the image of that maple-leafed moose head. A silver whistle was wrapped around his neck, his socks yanked up to his knees.

"All campers need to collect their cabin assignments," he shouted. "First meeting's in the amphitheater before dinner. Everybody hear me? Don't be late!"

Nobody seemed to be paying him any attention.

"I know you guys can hear me. *Don't. Be. Late.*"

## SURVIVAL STRATEGY #2:
### PINPOINT YOUR TROUBLEMAKERS.

Another bus, full of girls, pulled into the parking lot. They stared blankly back at us through their windows.

For a split second, I thought I saw Sully banging her fists against the glass.

I quickly pinched my eyes.

*Fight the fog, Spencer. Fight the fog fight the fog fight the fog . . .*

When I opened them, Sully was gone. Some girl I'd never

seen before was sitting in her place, hammering her hands against the window as their bus shifted into gear and shuttled around the bend.

*Where were they heading?*

All the boys must have been stuck on one side of the lake, while the girls were sequestered on the other. No intermingling.

Whoever came up with the idea to corral twenty teenage boys with behavioral problems into a single camp should have their head examined.

*Better yet—just lop it off and stack it on the totem pole.*

Scanning the campers, it struck me that everybody had the benchmark characteristics of a type A scallywag. *Cocky attitude. Crazy eyes. Scabs and bruises.*

Talk about a motley crew. We had been here for less than thirty seconds and already a couple campers had begun to scuffle.

That didn't take long, I thought.

I decided to give the boiling knot of bodies a wide berth. The kid in the midst of smashing his fist into another kid's face noticed my sidestep. He let his punching bag go.

"Hey," he said, walking my way. I acted as if I hadn't heard him. "Hey—*you.*"

He grabbed me by the shoulder and spun me around.

It was the kid from the seat in front of mine.

Mr. Brace-Face.

"You got off at the wrong bus stop, kid," he said. "The girl's camp is on the other side of the lake."

From between his chapped lips, the glint of metal shined in the sunlight.

"Thanks for the advice," I said. I even managed to smile back. "I can't help but feel like we may have gotten off on the wrong foot here. My name is—"

He hocked a loogie right into my face.

"You won't last a week," Brace-Face chuckled as he walked off, leaving me with a slender tendril of spit dangling off my nose. "Welcome to Camp New Blood."

## SURVIVAL STRATEGY #1:
### TRAVEL THE PATH OF LEAST RESISTANCE NO MATTER WHAT.

Cabin assignment in hand, I wandered down the footpath that connected the cabins like a centipede.

"Counselors will be performing a mandatory bag search." George had vanished, his voice now crackling over the camp's PA system. "Any cell phones or portable gaming devices hidden inside your belongings will be confiscated. You'll get them back at the end of the session. Don't think we won't find them!"

The intercom was exactly like your run-of-the-mill hookups you'd find in school, except the megaphones were bolted to each cabin's roof outside.

I paused on the path long enough to take in the towering pines over my head. Buried farther off into the woods, I spotted a clearing that looked like an archery range. I counted ten hay bales lined up alongside one another, a target sheet stapled to the front of each bundle of straw. I swear I saw one of the bull's-eyes blink.

My fellow campers ambled to their cabins while I remained standing in place, each one of them making sure to shove into my shoulder as they passed by.

"Excuse me."

"Coming through."

"Pardon *moi.*"

Keep it together, Spence, I thought. This summer is going to be different. It has to be. For Mom. For myself.

*From this point forward, I, Spencer Pendleton, hereby make the pledge to go down the straight and narrow.*

No more running away. No more trouble. No more rocking anybody's boat.

Or canoe, for that matter.

Farther down the main path, in another break between trees, I could see the sun reflecting off the glass-smooth surface of a lake.

I reached into my pocket and pulled out Mr. Simms's postcard. Holding it up, I compared the faded image with the real thing.

They were identical. Exact match.

*Welcome to Lake Wendigo.*

# BUNKMATES
# IN BEDLAM

I counted four cabins.

Cabin one, the main cabin situated just a stone's throw away from the parking lot, was the administrative office. Probably where Mr. Ponytail lived, while the junior counselors all bunked amongst us malfeasants.

The remaining three cabins were set farther into the woods.

Each cabin was arranged by age. Cabin two was crammed with the youngest kids, ten and under. It was a tinderbox of combustible campers with ADHD.

Let's call them—*The Preadolescent Piranhas.*

This land-roving pack tore through the campground like they had just snorted a Pixy Stix up each nostril. They stayed in tight formation, manically racing around in near lockstep syncopation. All eight seemed to communicate in a gibberish that only they could understand.

"Comingthroughwatchoutheadsupouttathewaygonnaeat you . . ."

I was sure that if I stepped too close, that jittery assembly of arms and legs (and teeth) would swarm around me and rip me to fleshy shreds.

The older kids were in cabin four, buried farther off into the woods away from the rest of us.

That left cabin three.

The ramshackle shack smack-dab in the center of camp was going to be my home for the next thirty days. It housed all the in-betweeners. We weren't the youngest boys on the block, but we were nowhere near the oldest guys here, either.

That made us—*The Middle Kids.*

A banner was slung over the door, upon which that maple-leafed moose head proclaimed:

# OUR HOME IS YOUR HOME AWAY FROM HOME!

"Here goes nothing." I took a puff from My Little Friend before stepping inside.

A row of bunk beds were positioned along one side. Their musty mattresses were thin and worn-down with time. A handful of hay with nails mixed in would probably have been more comfortable. The whole cabin had a mildewy smell to it.

*Nothing like a little mold to aggravate my asthma.*

Campers were unpacking, and unrolling their sleeping bags

over their beds. I eavesdropped on the conversation as I dragged my suitcase across the floor.

"Did you sneak a peak at Ali Lombardi on the girls' bus?"

"What about her?"

"I'm telling you, she's grown two cup sizes since last year."

"You're lying."

"See for yourself. Two bucks says she's a C-cup before summer ends."

As I passed their bunks, each boy quickly slid his hand over their mattress.

"Already taken."

"Taken."

"Keep moving, kiddo."

The broken record continued down the aisle, blocking me from their bunks.

"Taken."

"Taken."

"Taken."

I found a bed at the very back of the cabin, tucked far away from the rest of the boys. The bottom bunk was empty.

Looking at the mattress, I realized why.

A large yellow stain radiated out from its center.

*Please let that be lemonade.*

I leaned over and took a quick whiff.

*Definitely not lemonade.*

Looking up at the top bunk, I came face-to-face with a kid

clutching his suitcase—still unopened. Slightly overweight, his cheeks looked like they were stuffed full of food. Was he squirreling away a month's worth of meals for the summer or something?

"Guess you're stuck with the bed-wetters bed," he said. "Sorry."

"Should I even ask?"

"At the end of every summer, we pick one mattress and pee on it. When we come back, the last one to the cabin has to sleep in dried pee."

"You pee on it . . . *on purpose?*"

"Yup," he nodded and smiled. His cheek muscles flexed, bulking up beyond the normal proportions of a human being's mouth.

I hefted my suitcase onto the bottom bunk and gave a sigh. I would have been better off simply sleeping on the floor.

"First year, huh?" he asked, slightly easing his grip around his suitcase. "This is my third. Technically, it's my fourth, but I had to leave early last summer."

"What happened?"

"I bit one of the counselors."

"You . . . *what?*"

He smiled warmly. "Broke the skin and everything! He needed six stitches."

*I'm sharing a bunk with a human badger.*

"The doctors gave him a tetanus shot," he kept going. "Can

you believe that? *A tetanus shot!* Like I had rabies or something."

"Do you?" I couldn't help but ask.

He pondered the question for a moment. "I don't think so. . . ."

"They allowed you to come back?"

The kid shrugged his shoulders. "Got nowhere else to go."

I unzipped my suitcase. There, on the other side of the flap, Sully's well-worn black-and-white missing flyer stared back at me.

My bunkmate leaned his head over the edge of the bed. "Who's that?"

"Just somebody I used to know."

I slipped her flyer into the wooden framework of the upper bunk.

"My name's Charles," my bunk-badger interrupted.

"Hey," I mumbled. I wasn't in the mood for making friends.

All I wanted was to stay out of everybody's way.

"Looks like somebody wet his bed already," someone said over my shoulder.

I looked up to discover Brace-Face standing at the foot of our bunk. Scanning his hands, I saw that his knuckles were laced with a fresh set of scrapes.

*How many fistfights has he gotten into today?*

"This is the middle kids' cabin," Charles said. "You're up with the older kids this year."

"Mind your own business," Brace-Face muttered. "I just

wanted to pay a visit to our fresh fish here, and see how he was getting along on his first day."

He leaned in and peeled his lips back to reveal those thick train-track braces. Flecks of food were still stuck to the brackets. I got a good whiff of his breath.

Not pleasant. Personal hygiene wasn't a top priority for this kid.

Brace-Face cupped his hand behind his rear end and farted into it, then brought it back up for me to shake.

"My name's Capone. What's yours?"

"Holden Caulfield," I said, opting out of taking his hand.

"Rude, isn't he?" Capone said. "That's no way to make friends on your first day at camp."

"I think I might've touched some poison oak earlier," I lied. "Don't want to spread any itchiness around, you know?"

Our cabin was suddenly full of older campers. They waltzed in without an invitation, sifting through suitcases to see if there was anything worth taking.

Before I knew it, I was boxed into my bunk.

"Check out all the books," one older camper said. It looked as if one of his eyes had latched on to my open suitcase while the other stared me down.

It took me a couple blinks to realize he had a lazy eye.

He was right. I had packed more books than clothes.

Lazy Eye slipped his hand into my suitcase and snatched my copy of *The Outsiders*. It happened so fast, I had to do a double take just to make sure I had actually seen him take it.

# FILE #16: SALVATORE "CAPONE" GRIMALDI

Capone is Camp New Leaf's resident lunkhead. The counselors have been stuck with him every year since he was ten. His parents can't stand having him around the house, so they dump him here each summer.

Capone has what you would call a "habitual pattern of maladjusted behavior." Excessive aggression. A fondness for destruction. He broke every window in his house with his bare fists simply because his mother told him to turn off the TV and go play outside. He was six at the time.

There's a rumor going around camp that Capone has beaten up three different counselors during his tenure at Camp New Leaf. He supposedly broke one's nose. Whether that's true or not remains to be seen, but most counselors seem to keep their distance from Capone at whatever cost.

Medication: Chlorapentaline, Verchlonodine, Titmouzium

"Hey!" I sprung out from my bunk. "Give that back!"

"Or what?"

"Or I'll . . ."

Before I could retaliate with some quick-witted quip, Charles, teeth bared, leapt off the top bunk and landed directly on Lazy Eye, snapping at his face.

Lazy Eye lifted his arm up to protect himself, and Charles didn't think twice before sinking his teeth into Lazy Eye's forearm.

"Get him off me!"

Capone grabbed Charles's head and slipped his fingers around his lower jaw, prying his mandibles apart. He snaked his pinkies into Charles's nostrils for traction.

"Can't hold on for long," he strained. "I'm losing my grip!"

Capone's fingers slid down Charles's jaw, until . . .

*SNAP!*

Capone screamed at the top of his lungs. "*Yeeeeeeeeeeeeaaaa!*"

That was all the invitation my cabinmates needed to start punching.

In a flash, the whole cabin was in on the fight. What had started as a scuffle between four kids quickly grew. Ten. Fifteen. Twenty. Older campers pounded on the in-betweeners, punching and kicking just for the fun of it.

There was blood in the water now, which only lured in more sharks to this free-for-all. The whole camp was here, and everybody was happy to pitch in a fist.

The Piranhas rushed in and immediately swarmed around the first camper they found. One second, this kid was standing on his own two feet—the next, he was enveloped by eight gnashing adolescents, all of them gnawing on a different limb.

"Yummyyummyinthetummyyummyyummyinthetummy."

Don't get involved, Spencer, I thought. Don't do something you'll regret.

I pressed my back against the wall and surveyed the room, taking in the tumult.

That's when I saw something that froze the air in my lungs.

There. On the other side of the cabin.

An acne-addled camper was full-on eye-knifing me.

I know this kid, I said to myself.

A name popped into my head. A name I hadn't spoken out loud in months.

*Compass?*

It couldn't be. The last time I laid eyes on him, he had just laced Greenfield Middle's lunch with enough funky fungus to create a tidal wave of diarrhea.

*Impossible.*

Doctor Lobotomy would call this "the transference of figments of my imagination onto others."

I'd say I was seeing things.

I squeezed my eyes shut until I saw stars behind my eyelids.

This had to be a hallucination. There was no other explanation. I had taken a dose of my medication that morning, and the fog had washed over my head for the whole bus ride.

Now, from somewhere deep within that dense cloud, my fevered mind had conjured up this blast from my past.

*Fight the fog fight the fog fight the fog fight the fog fight the fog . . .*

I counted to ten before opening my eyes.

Compass—or whoever he was—was gone. In his place, I found Capone standing directly in front of me.

"Peekaboo," he said as he grabbed my collar and yanked me into the fracas. His braces budded from his lips as he pulled his fist back.

*"Hey, hey, hey!"* A scrawny guy with two or three whiskers on his chin popped through the door. He wore a New Leaf T-shirt, emblazoned with a maple-leafed moose head. He was too old to be a camper. His wire-rimmed glasses suggested he should be checking out library books.

"Break it up, break it up!" he shouted.

Capone wasn't listening. Nobody was.

This pencil pusher forced his way through the vortex of violence, clasping Capone's fist before it could connect with my face, and tried to pull him off of me.

"Enough, Capone!"

When that didn't seem to work, he plucked up the silver whistle hanging from his neck and gave a good blow.

The fight instantaneously stopped.

Capone let me go and everyone stepped back, out of breath, ever-so-slightly relieved to call it quits.

"Come on, guys," the counselor started in. "This type of behavior is really unacceptable. Let's focus that aggression on something more productive, okay?"

"Like smashing your face in!" Lazy Eye spat at Charles.

Another round of combat erupted. Lazy Eye kicked Charles in the shin, sending him buckling over. Charles sank his teeth into Lazy Eye's ankle.

"*Whoa, Thomas, whoa.*" The counselor blew into his whistle and waited for the campers to calm down. "Got that all out of your system? You sure? Good. Most of you know who I am. For those who don't, I am Stan the Man. As in, I am 'The Man.'"

Nobody seemed convinced.

"You've got two minutes before we meet in the amphitheater. I don't care how many years you've been here, you've gotta hear George go through the rules again. Remember—*Rules are signposts that help us navigate our way down the highway of life.* So get a move on!"

Charles was on the floor, clutching his shin. I held out my hand.

"You okay?"

"Everybody's got to show off on the first day," he said, taking my hand. I pulled him from the floor.

"Be careful," I said. "Looks like you took some pretty big licks there."

Charles gave me his best puppy-pit-bull eyes. "Do you think maybe you and me could go to the amphitheater together?"

"Look, kid . . ." I sighed. "I don't know how to say this nicely, so I'm just gonna tell it to you straight: just because we're bunkmates doesn't make us friends."

"Why not?"

"I'm bad news. Trust me. You're better off making friends with somebody else here."

Charles shook his head and grinned. The grin grew, until he bared his teeth.

"You don't get it yet, do you?" he asked. A bit of blood glistened on his lips. Whose blood was anybody's guess.

"What's there to get?"

"Everybody's bad news here," he said. "Most of us are worse news than you."

# THE SACRIFICIAL ALTAR

## DAY ONE: 1400 HOURS

The amphitheater was a dug-out crater with a fire pit at its heart. Five concentric rings of logs circled around the sloping sides of the cavity.

I had a bad feeling about this place right away. This had to be where the counselors made their offerings to the summer solstice gods.

All the campers squeezed together on their logs while the Piranhas turned the amphitheater into their personal racetrack.

"Comingthroughwatchoutheadsupherewecome."

You could tell who was new. They kept to themselves.

Like me.

I kept my eyes open for Compass. His pockmarks would make him hard to miss. That's if I had even seen him in the first place. I was weighing the possibility when the hairs on the back of my neck sprung up. I slowly turned my head to find nothing but a canopy of pine trees. Their leaves rustled in the wind like cheerleader pom-poms.

Charles squeezed in next to me. "Is this log taken?"

"Is now, I guess."

"Who?" Charles turned his head and looked over his shoulder.

"Uh—you."

"Oh, yeah." He laughed, finally getting it. "Right. Sorry."

Charles smiled at me, as if he were simply happy to have somebody to share a log with. I caught a glimpse of his razor teeth and wondered if I should be worried.

George stood before the fire pit and cleared his throat. A whistle attached to the lanyard around his neck gleamed like some kind of magical talisman. He was flanked by Stan the Man and three younger counselors.

I was sitting close enough to the front to overhear one of the counselors—the one with a patch of peach fuzz stretched across his upper lip—grumbling.

"I can't believe I'm stuck babysitting again," Peach Fuzz muttered. "You want to trade off with me?"

"Not a chance," Stan the Man said. "Cabin two's all yours, man."

"I'm slipping valium into their marshmallows all summer long."

George scanned the crowd before blowing into his whistle.

"*Helloooooo*, campers!"

# FILE #7: CHARLES SANDERS

Charles had been a punching bag ever since he was five. He wasn't fast or tough enough to stick up for himself. All the older kids targeted him before his baby teeth had even started to fall out. So, once he finally got his adult teeth, he started a regiment of eating raw carrots for every meal, masticating his day away until his jaw was reinforced with a thick strip of muscle and sinew.

Charles had the puffiest cheeks you'd ever seen, his buccinators bulked beyond belief. Adults thought he looked adorable, always oohing and aahing at him and pinching his cheeks—but Charles's iron-jawed mouth might as well have been a roulette wheel. The moment it opened, you were gambling your life away, until—crack—his mandibles snapped, sealing his teeth together like a bear trap. Once his masseter muscles cinched, there was no unlocking them.

If Charles couldn't fight back the bullies with his fists, he'd bite back. Hard. And he wasn't afraid of breaking skin, either. Whenever he was backed into a corner and all else failed, he would simply sink his teeth into the closest limb and hold on for dear life.

Charles ended up getting into more trouble for defending himself. Suddenly he became the tormenter, and his bullies the victims. He sent more kids to the hospital for stitches than any bully ever did.

## Medication: Rabidium, Cujopentantaline

Everyone responded snarkily, as if this were a well-rehearsed routine that they were all bored with—"*Helloooooooo*, George."

"Welcome to Camp New Leaf! I see a lot of familiar faces here, which is great. Glad to have you back for another summer. And I see a few *new* folks here, too. What do you say we give a big ol' Camp New Leaf welcome to all the newbies out there? *Helloooooo*, newbies!"

"*Helloooooo*, newbies."

*Newbies*. No matter where I go, I'm always going to be the rookie.

"One of our goals here at New Leaf is to work toward strengthening your sense of self-worth," George continued. "We want to challenge you with new and exciting experiences. We want to help develop your courage and confidence. Build up your self-esteem and leadership abilities, while exploring the wonders of nature."

Translation: Camp New Leaf is a touchy-feely therapeutic camp for kids who would snap your finger in half if you point at them.

"Camp New Leaf is over three hours by car from the nearest city. That's over *one hundred fifty miles* from civilization! That means we can leave our city lives behind and immerse ourselves in the wonders of nature."

Translation: There's no point trying to escape.

"There's only one phone at camp and it's in my office," George continued. "All campers can call home once a week on Sundays or in case of an emergency."

It was quickly dawning on me how cut off from the rest of the world we were.

And I thought house arrest had been bad. For the next thirty days, I was completely stranded.

"At New Leaf, we want to give you a summer you'll remember. The memories you make here will last you a lifetime. Heck—most campers will beg to come back!"

"Beg to?" Capone said under his breath. "More like they're forced to."

*Took the words right out of my mouth, Capone. . . .*

"Camp New Leaf is situated alongside Lake Wendigo," George said, ignoring Capone. "We are separated into 'brother' and 'sister' camps."

At the mention of our sister camp, a chorus of *ooooohs* rose up.

"Rule one: *Don't bother the girls' camp.* Got me? If you're caught sneaking out for a little kissy-kissy, you'll get . . ."

"Booted?" I interrupted, full of hope.

"Sorry—no one gets the 'boot' here." George scanned the crowd to pinpoint who'd said it. "This lake's big enough that we can all call it home."

Then, there it was again. That *feeling.*

I couldn't shake the sensation I was being spied on. I would've sworn there was someone out there in the woods watching me.

No. From across the amphitheater.

An older camper.

Where had I seen those crazy eyes before?

The answer came in a flash.

He was leaner since the last time I laid eyes on him, but his sunburned cheeks couldn't hide those freckles. He still had that sponge of curly orange hair atop his head.

And those wild eyes.

*There's no way that's him, Spencer. You're acting mental.*

I pinched my eyes shut and counted down from ten. When I reached zero, I opened them up again and—

Sporkboy was still there.

Looking at me.

Smiling.

"So whaddya say, campers?" A sunny can-do attitude seeped through George's voice. "*Heeeeere's to . . .*"

". . . Camp New Leaf."

"Come on, now. You can do better than that! *Heeeeeeere's to . . .*"

". . . Camp New Leaf!"

"Now that's more like it! One more time! *Heeeeeere's to . . .*"

". . . *CAMP NEW LEAF!*"

# POOP
# THERAPY

*The Last Stand of a Balding Man.*

Examining George—and his ponytail—up close, I could see that his widow's peak retreated past his ears. It looked as if somebody had gripped him by the back of his head and yanked so hard, all of his hair now hung on in the rear.

I really should break the bad news to him: *Really poor choice in hairstyle.*

But first: Poop therapy.

Sorry. *Group* therapy.

The pamphlet called these sessions "round-table chats in an open-air environment." Any kid worth their neuroses knew better.

Time to "share our feelings."

Time to "explore our emotions."

Time to take a nap.

The Middle Kids from cabin three all sat cross-legged in a circle. We had been told to stay behind while the other campers broke off into their own age groups.

I had watched Sporkboy slip off with the older campers and was about to make my way through the crowd and follow him, when George blocked my exit with a sunny can-do smile.

"Just where do we think we're going?" he asked.

"Nowhere. Just taking in the wonders of nature."

"I'm gonna have to keep an eye on you, aren't I?"

"Me?" I shook my head. "Nope—no, sir. You can keep your eyes to yourself."

Deep within the woods, a duet of birds chirped back and forth. The scent of the surrounding pines lingered in the air, filling my lungs.

The freshness was beginning to freak me out a bit. It was almost a little *too* fresh.

"What a beautiful day at Camp New Leaf, huh?" George squeezed into our circle, looking more eager to be sitting here than anyone else. "It's so great to see so many familiar faces again! Mason—welcome back!"

A kid in a long-sleeved hoodie tugged on his frayed cuffs, pulling them down until they swallowed his hands. ". . . Hey."

This definitely wasn't sweatshirt weather. It was too hot to be wearing a hoodie.

"How have things been?"

"Okay, I guess." Mason busied himself with a pair of sticks.

"Mind me asking how many *reversions* you've had since last year?"

"Twelve," he mumbled. "Maybe thirteen."

"A baker's dozen!" George seemed pleased. "I'd say that's an improvement. That deserves a hand. Everybody—let's give Mason a little New Leaf cheer."

George started clapping. Charles joined in, then stopped when he realized nobody else was applauding.

Mason just started rubbing his sticks together, faster and faster. Blond-haired and blue-eyed, he looked like your average everyday bored-out-of-his-gourd suburban troublemaker. Probably his biggest problem was he had a little too much time on his hands. Nothing out of the ordinary there. But peeking out from beneath the collar of his sweatshirt, I caught a glimpse of discolored tissue.

It was craggy, like lava rock.

I lost myself in the fibrous flesh wrapping around Mason's neck, then suddenly discovered it snaking around his wrists as well.

George cleared his throat, drawing my attention back to the circle.

"Anybody know why we sit in a circle?" He waited for an answer.

Nobody offered one.

"It's because no one's in charge here."

*Is this guy for real?*

# FILE #12: MASON REYNOLDS

Mason fell in love with the kitchen oven his mother cooked on when he was nine years old. She would slip a casserole in, and in a matter of thirty minutes at three hundred and fifty degrees, it came out transformed. The intense heat had turned it into something new. Something special. So, one day, when his mother wasn't looking, he opened the oven and reached his hand inside, hoping to harness that fire for himself. What he got instead was a second-degree burn all along the fingers and palm of his left hand.

Mason started off frying ants with a magnifying glass, and quickly graduated onto his first box of matches. Now, there's no holding him back. . . .

Word around the campfire is that Mason burned down the last three houses he's lived in, and apparently, he set his school's mascot on fire during a pep rally . . . while there was a kid still inside it.
(He got out alive.)

At the beginning of every summer, the counselors at New Leaf have to check his pockets for lighters. Each morning at breakfast, he's frisked before sitting down at the mess hall table, just in case.

Medication: Protasoline, Kerosipitrol, Pretrotaz

"This is a conversation, people," George continued. "You don't have a conversation when one person stands in front of a class and talks down to everyone else."

*God, I just want to tug that ponytail of his. . . .*

"A circle is our bond, okay? It links us together. . . ."

*Just one quick yank . . .*

"We are a fellowship here. We are one."

My hand lifted from my side. I could feel myself slowly reaching for that ponytail.

So much for self-restraint.

George turned to me and noticed my raised hand. "You don't need to raise your hand to ask a question. We're not in class."

"Sorry," I said, lowering my hand. All heads turned toward me. "I just want to be clear that I'm hearing you correctly. . . . Are you saying you're *not* our leader?"

"I'd like to think of myself as more of a moderator," George replied after taking his sweet time to mull it over. "A facilitator for our group discussion."

"So . . . if you're not our leader, then who says we have to be here?"

George hesitated. "Well—I'm the one who says you have to be here."

"But you're not our leader."

"Theoretically, I am."

"But you just said you're not."

"Well—technically, yes. But—*conceptually*, no."

"I'm confused."

"I'm still in charge of overseeing the camp, but *here*, when we get together for our afternoon discussions—"

"You mean therapy?"

George's eyes tightened. "This is your first summer here, isn't it?"

"Yessir."

"For our *afternoon discussions*, I try to step back from my official status and become one of the guys. Just because I'm a counselor at this summer camp doesn't mean I can't have a little fun too."

"You mean prison camp."

As in, a full-blown gulag in the tick-infested great outdoors.

George paused, then nodded to the woods. "See those trees?"

I turned to look. Then turned back and nodded.

"Does that look like a prison to you?"

"A prison doesn't need to look like a prison to be a prison," I said.

"Very interesting." George checked something off on his clipboard. "You can go."

My eyes widened. I turned to Charles. He shrugged his shoulders.

"If you feel like breaking out of this beautiful, serene *prison*," George extended his arm, palm upward, as if to present the woods to me. "Have at it."

I kept to my log, unsure of what to do.

"What's wrong, Mr . . ." George scanned his clipboard. "Pendleton? I thought you wanted to escape? Here's your chance."

I didn't move.

"I don't blame you one bit," he said. "With over fifty miles of woods between you and the nearest town. We trust you to real-ize that *there's nowhere for you to go*."

How do you break out of a prison that doesn't have any bars?

I was willing to find out.

I stood up. "Catch you guys later. . . ."

I had taken only two steps before I heard a branch snap.

Scanning the woods, I spotted a deer.

At least I thought it was a deer. I saw something with antlers walking between the trees.

For a split second, no more than a single synaptic misfire in my chemically clouded mind, I could have sworn that deer was walking upright on its hind legs.

A memory of a hoodied reindeer from Greenfield Middle suddenly popped into my mind, only these antlers seemed real.

I turned my head back to the circle, *"Do you see that?"*

"See what . . . ?"

I scanned the woods once more, but the antlers were gone.

"I just—I think I just saw—"

A bird chirped overhead. There was something familiar to the ululation.

Something *human*.

"You guys hear that?" I asked, my chest tensing. "Tell me you heard that, okay?"

"That's the sound of Mother Nature," George offered. "Guess you don't get much of that in the city?"

The first chirp was met with another, coming from deeper in the woods.

It sounded like they were communicating.

Telling each other to close in.

You're imagining things, Spencer, I thought to myself. There's no way that could be—

Another chirp.

"Spencer?" George asked.

Then another.

"Earth to Spencer . . ."

I stepped back from the trees. *Slowly.* Safety in numbers. Returning to the circle, I noticed most campers weren't even looking at me. Except for Charles. Paranoid behavior probably wasn't anything new at New Leaf. Mason continued to rub his sticks together.

"Glad you decided to stay," George said. "Why don't you start off our discussion today?"

"There's nothing to discuss." I focused my attention on the woods.

"The first step toward making progress is to claim responsibility for the things we've done."

Another chirp.

Louder now.

"Maybe you could explain to the rest of us why you want to run away so badly. Perhaps it has something to do with your parents separating?"

"Can we please not talk about my parents?" I shot back.

"Why not?"

"Because it's none of your business, that's why."

"Sometimes we do things solely for the purpose of drawing attention to us," George said. "Now, I have read some pretty wild stories from your therapist. . . ."

"I don't need a therapist." I shot him a glance before turning my attention back to the woods. "The court is making me go see a therapist."

"I'm not accusing you of needing a therapist, Spencer. What I'm saying is, rather than using your imagination to paint a vivid portrait of other runaways—"

"I didn't make them up."

Another twitter. This one sounded nearer.

The chirps were closing in.

Something's wrong here, Spence, I thought. Something's about to happen.

"If you want people to listen to what you have to say, you don't have to—"

I leapt to my feet. "They're real. *They're here!* We've got to go!"

"Spencer, please . . ."

"They're coming!"

"Who?"

"The Tribe, that's who! They're surrounding us right now! I can hear them communicating with each other—"

Just then, a pair of robins perched themselves on a branch above my head.

I took a step back, realizing how crazy I must have just sounded.

*But I could've sworn they sounded just like . . .*

I couldn't even finish the thought.

*Like what, exactly?*

An infinitesimal part of me refused to let go, believing even now that the Tribe was out there, somewhere in the woods, circling the camp at that very moment, only seconds away from raiding our group therapy session.

"I think I'm going to recommend we increase your Chlorofornil for a couple days." A sense of superiority saturated George's words. "At least until we can communicate more clearly. How's that sound?"

I stared George down. "Something bad is going to happen here."

"Are you . . . threatening me, Spencer?"

"No. I'm *warning* you."

"I think you'll find threats don't go over so well with me."

I could feel my hand tighten.

I wanted to throttle him.

I wanted to—

A slender thread of smoke rose up from the patch of pine needles before Mason's feet, then puffed into a plume. He sat back and marveled at his handiwork.

I could've sworn I caught a glimpse of a match burning deep in his pupils.

George jumped up and quickly did a soft-shoe dance in his leather sandals to stomp out the flames.

"It's okay, it's okay—I got this one! No worries, gang! I got it!"

Turning back, I took in the endless stretch of pines.

I could cut through these trees, make my way back to the service road, and eventually reach the highway. From there, I just had to flag down a car, give them a sob story about getting lost in the woods and—*BAM:* I'd be home before nightfall.

But which home would I be running to, exactly?

Which one would take me?

# ONE FLEW OVER THE CUCKOO'S MESS

alking through the doors to the mess hall, I was immediately greeted by a huge moose.

Its head, that is.

Camp New Leaf's official mascot was mounted directly above the main entrance. Its shabby antlers had been painted green to resemble leaves.

That animal had seen better days, for sure.

Its fur had begun to peel back. I spotted a spider crawling out from one of its cobwebbed nostrils.

I had no appetite. All I wanted was to sit and keep an eye out for unwanted company.

I don't care how paranoid I was coming off—this camp was closing in on me.

Scanning the older kids' table for a sign of Sporkboy, or even Compass, I spotted a camper towering over the rest. His back was to me.

His awfully brawny back.

There's no way. *Absolutely no way.*

Shaking my head, I tried to shake the six-foot mirage from my mind.

*Fight the fog fight the fog fight the fog fight the fog fight*—

To heck with this, I said to myself. I'm tired of hallucinating. If that really is who I think it is, there's only one way to find out.

I walked over and stood behind him.

When he didn't turn around, I cleared my throat.

Nothing.

So I reached up and tapped the skyscraper on his shoulder.

That got his attention.

He stood up and my eyes leveled with his chest. I had to crane my neck back just to take a look at him.

"What . . ." I started, swallowed. "What are you doing here?"

Yardstick stared me down with an unimpressed look on his face.

"Going to camp?"

His hair was twisted into tiny nano-dreadlocks that coiled around his scalp. One eyebrow lifted with a bit of attitude—which was a surprise, considering the Yardstick I knew had been so cripplingly bashful, he'd hardly even meet your gaze.

"Do I even know you?" There was a confidence in his voice that hadn't been there before. All that shyness seemed to have evaporated.

"You can't fool me," I said. "I know who you are."

Yardstick just shook his head.

"Stop acting like I'm crazy!" I shouted. "I'm not crazy!"

The mess hall went quiet just then.

Turning around, I realized all eyes were on me. "Do you see this kid?" I pointed at Yardstick. "He's one of them! One of the . . ."

My voice faded.

I *was* acting crazy.

I cleared my throat. I turned back to Yardstick. "I don't know what you're doing here, but I would appreciate it if you stopped messing with my head. . . ."

"Whatever, man."

I stepped back from the table.

*He's toying with you, Spencer.*

They all were. First, Compass. Then Sporkboy. Now Yardstick. They had embedded themselves into New Leaf. Sleepaway camp sleeper cells.

The Middle Kids from cabin three were sitting a few tables away.

Charles shoveled a plastic forkful of coleslaw into his mouth and spat it into the air over his head, then looked at me and smiled. "Spencer! Over here!"

I chose a seat directly across from Stan the Man.

"Not hungry?" he asked as he brushed the diced cabbage out of his hair.

"What's on the menu?"

"Tofu dogs, veggie burgers, brown rice, gluten-free tempeh . . ."

"Seriously?"

"The healthier the stuff you put into your body, the healthier the stuff you get out."

"You mean number two?"

"No," Stan the Man said. "*Vibes*. Positive energy."

"Who cooks this crap?"

"You do."

I couldn't help but laugh. "You definitely don't want me cooking."

"Every camper here is assigned a job," Stan the Man said. "The older campers usually get kitchen duty, but don't be too surprised if you get dish detail."

Stan the Man pointed to the area directly behind a row of steam tables.

The first thing I noticed was a wire-meshed hairnet swallowing a huge orange afro. Sporkboy looked up and, giving me his biggest grin, ladled a spoonful of brown rice onto Capone's dinner tray.

Leaning over the table, I whispered, "You've got to believe me. The whole camp is in danger."

"How so?"

"I've been followed. . . ."

"Followed?"

"I know this sounds crazy, but there's a gang of kids stalking me. I think—I *know* they've tracked me down."

"Hmm-hmm." He smiled, rather agreeably—but Stan was giving me *That Look*.

"I believe you, Spencer," Charles offered.

"Spencer . . ." Stan the Man's voice sounded very even. Calm. "I hate to say it, but you're sounding a little . . . *delusional*. I read over your file and I think . . ."

"You've read my file, too?" I interrupted. "What's it say?

I could picture it in my head:

## FILE #20: SPENCER AUSTIN PENDLETON

What can I say? I'm a runner. Always have been, always will be. Which is ironic, if you think about it, given that the one time I could have run away for good and joined the Tribe, I didn't bolt—and ended up getting in the most trouble I've ever landed in before in my entire life. And believe me, I've gotten into plenty of trouble: Expelled for setting my science class on fire. Attacked vice principal with stapler. Poked a teacher in the eye with pencil. Expelled a second time for food poisoning fellow classmates.

Did I also mention I'm a bit of a fibber? I've told more tales than both of the Grimm brothers. Hans Christian Andersen hasn't got anything on me.

Now I'm serving a six-month sentence of house arrest. My parents are separated. Currently living with father. Therapy once a week.

But now I've got an itch to run that I'm just about ready to scratch. . . .

Medication: Chlorofornil

"Spencer." Stan the Man held out his hands. "Calm down."

Something wasn't right. I couldn't put my finger on it at first. "You're not a regular camp counselor—are you?"

"Caught me." Stan raised his hands. "I'm actually a grad student."

"You're a *student*?"

"Aren't we all?"

"Studying what?"

"You, actually. I'm a developmental psychology major. I'm focusing my thesis on adolescent behavioral problems. You kids will be the basis for my paper."

"I'm some guinea pig to you?"

"All I do is observe."

"What's there to observe?"

"Everything." Stan stood up. "Enough chitchat. You've got to come with me."

He escorted me over to the dinner line. At its end sat Peach Fuzz with a tray of sip-size paper cups. Each cup was marked with a different name.

Peering inside, I saw that the cups held a multicolored cluster of pills.

Red pills. Green pills. Blue pills.

Horse pills. Gel caps.

Hoppers. Poppers.

Animal-shaped chewables.

Breath mints.

Every kind of medication under the sun.

"What are those?"

"Your prescriptions," Peach Fuzz said.

I zeroed in on the cup with my name written across its side.

So this is how the counselors were supposed to keep us in line. Our own specially designed chemical cocktail.

"Here," Stan the Man said, picking up the cup with my name on it. "Wash 'em down with some orange juice."

"I'm okay, thanks." I shook my head as I slowly back-stepped away.

"Pendleton," Peach Fuzz muttered. "Either take your medication or we *make* you take it."

"You really need to work on your bedside manner."

"It's for your own good, Spencer," Stan the Man said.

"Good luck getting me to swallow those."

"There are *other ways*," Peach Fuzz said.

I couldn't help but laugh. "How's that?"

Peach Fuzz cleared his throat. "These pills are going into your body one way or another—in one end, *or in the other end*."

I took the cup. My pills were Christmas-colored, green and red.

"Swallow," Peach Fuzz ordered.

I cricked my neck back and poured the pills into my mouth.

"That wasn't so hard, was it?" Peach Fuzz gave me a smarmy grin. "Now open wide."

I spat the pills straight into his face.

I was ready to bolt for the door, but Peach Fuzz grabbed my shoulder. He and Stan the Man each took an arm and held on.

"Suppository it is," Peach Fuzz said.

"Let go!"

Stan the Man picked my pills off the floor and presented them to me. "Don't make this harder than it has to be, Spencer. Swallow this time."

"There's a hair stuck to it. . . ."

"Just do it, Spencer."

I clamped my mouth shut. Lips pursed, I shook my head.

"Don't swallow!" Capone shouted from the older campers' table.

"Don't swallow, don't swallow!" Charles parroted.

Peach Fuzz pinched my nose.

Other campers picked up on the chant, until the entire mess hall echoed—"Don't swallow! Don't swallow! Don't swallow!"

*Just hold your breath, Spence. Whatever you do, don't open your mouth.*

The air in my lungs started to sizzle.

"Don't swallow! Don't swallow! Don't . . ."

My mouth burst open. Peach Fuzz popped my prescription in.

". . . swallow."

Peach Fuzz pressed his palm over my mouth until I swallowed. I gulped for emphasis.

"Good," Peach Fuzz nodded. "Now say *aaah*."

I opened my mouth and rolled around my tongue.

Empty.

"Feeling better already," I mumbled, and shuffled back to my table.

Lazy Eye made sure none of the counselors were eavesdropping before walking over to my table.

"*Psst.*" He nudged me in the gut. "I'm Thomas."

He held out his hand. I thought he wanted me to shake it.

"Hand 'em over."

"I don't know what you're talking about," I muttered.

"You might be good enough to fool them, but you're not good enough to fool me. Put your bottom lip down."

This kid Thomas was good. *Real good.* His lazy eye darted all over the room, allowing him to look in two separate directions at once. I could tell he was scanning the cafeteria to see if any of the counselors had noticed what he was up to. His lanky profile made him look more like a stretched-out shadow than an actual person. Even when he was sitting next to me, it almost felt like he had just left, while his shadow stayed behind.

He wasn't there even when he was.

I made sure no one was looking my way before digging my finger behind my bottom lip and fishing out the pills.

"Why should I give you my meds?"

"I'll cut you in," he whispered. "Sixty-forty."

*"Cut me in?"*

"Fine—fifty-fifty! But it better be the brand-name stuff. No generic."

"What are you talking about?"

"Our parents don't trust us with our scripts, so the counselors monitor our meds. Your dad filled out a form with your medication history on it. *Georgie Porgie* keeps it on file in the head office. At every meal, they dole out whatever dosage is written on that form. But . . ."

Thomas grinned, wriggling his eyebrows.

"But—*what?*"

"A business-minded man such as myself can sell all kinds of meds to other campers. You need a boost to get you through the day? I'm your man."

# FILE #8: THOMAS WELLS

Keep an eye on your stuff around him. Possessions have a funny way of disappearing when he's nearby. You name it, he'll take it. . . .

When he was seven, Thomas's parents found a stockpile of stolen goods in their attic. Years' worth of missing items were stored in piles—silverware, fine China, jewelry, other children's toys.

Thomas was first caught shoplifting at age nine. He's been arrested four times since then. His mother doesn't take him grocery shopping anymore. If she has to, she makes sure to empty his pockets before checking out.

Thomas's crowning achievement last year had been to snitch the car keys of every last counselor. He'd hidden them in a hollowed-out tree trunk. It wasn't until all the campers had boarded their buses and were heading back home that George and the rest realized that they were completely stranded, all thanks to Thomas's quick fingers.

Medication: Surveilaprol, Stikifingertine

Thomas's lazy eye scanned the room while his other eye remained on me. When he was sure the coast was clear he pulled a tackle box from beneath his seat.

Opening it, the top portion revealed an assortment of . . .

". . . School supplies?"

"You can never be too careful," he winked.

He pulled out the top shelf to reveal a hidden compartment underneath.

"We got your stimulants," Thomas wound up his sales pitch. "Or how about antidepressants? We've got everything under the sun—except for Chlorofornil. You're the only one here with that prescription."

"Lucky me."

Throughout our meal, I watched kids walk up behind Thomas and whisper into his ear. He'd fish through his tackle kit and make the exchange under the table.

By the time dinner was finished, Thomas had raked in nearly fifty bucks.

"You're really making a killing," I said.

"That rusty-headed loony from the lunch line?" Thomas must've meant Sporkboy. "He's my biggest customer. Cleaned me out of my Valium before anyone else could ask."

"Why would he need so many?"

"Sleep, I guess." Thomas shrugged. "He's got enough now to put an elephant into a coma, if he wanted to."

# CANNIBALS AROUND THE CAMPFIRE

There wasn't another tribal sighting for the rest of the night.

"All you younger campers must report back to your bunks in ten minutes," George's tinny voice crackled over the PA. "Hope you get a good night's sleep! See you bright and early. Campers from cabins three and four, please meet in the amphitheater."

Peach Fuzz had to corral all of the Piranhas for their bedtime. Easier said than done. Whenever he caught up to the pack of rabid preadolescents, they would burst apart and scatter.

"Runrunrunasfastasyoucanrunrunrunasfastasyoucan."

They would reconnect as soon as they'd put enough distance between themselves and the hyperventilating Peach Fuzz.

"Game over, guys," he said with an abrupt yawn. "Time for . . . bed."

A bonfire was waiting for the older campers, its flames casting an orange glow over the logs. Stan the Man broke out a bag of marshmallows and we were each given a stick to roast our own.

George pulled out an acoustic guitar. "Who remembers this golden oldie?" He asked as he strummed away, leading the boys through a halfhearted sing-along:

*"I feel goood, breathing in the cleeeean air. . . . My mind feels cleeeeear, happy and awaaaaaaaaare."*

Now it was time to get down to business.

Ghost stories.

"Does anybody here know how Lake Wendigo got its name?" George asked.

Nobody answered.

"I'm sure you all saw the totem pole when you pulled into the parking lot earlier today, yes? Well, every totem pole tells a story, and the tale told by our very own is of a cannibalistic spirit called . . . *the Wendigo.*"

"This lake was named after a man-eating demon?" I asked. "You'd think people would want to name it after a happier spirit."

George double-taked me, his mouth half open, as if he were trying to decide whether or not he wanted to respond.

He let this one slide.

"The winters here were harsh," he continued, his eyes lingering on me for a second before returning to the rest. "Food would grow scarce the lower the temperature dropped. People starved to death. But there was a fate far worse than famine. Something much more painful than dying of hunger."

George scanned his eyes over the crowd. He took in a deep breath.

"The Wendigo was nothing but skin and bones. Its ribs raised up from its flesh. Its eyes sunk deep into its sockets, its thin lips pulled back over a row of crooked teeth. Some say it even had antlers, like a deer."

If my mind wasn't so zonked on prescriptions half of the day, I'd say I had seen something just like the Wendigo that very afternoon.

"It was almost human, but not quite. Half man, half animal— *all hunger.*"

"Sounds like Charles," Capone chuckled.

"Take that back," Charles insisted.

"The Wendigo would whisper your name when your stomach had shriveled down to the size of a prune. It would offer you a choice: Let the Wendigo possess you and make you stronger . . . or die of starvation."

Charles raised his hand. "Most people picked possession?"

Capone poked Charles in the stomach with his roasting stick.

"What?" Charles asked. "I was just curious. . . ."

Capone jabbed him again.

"Stop."

And again.

"I said *stop.*" Charles stood, limbering up his jaw and glowering at Capone.

Capone threw his stick into the fire and got up to face Charles, baring his own metal-covered teeth.

I grabbed Charles's wrist. He looked at me—and for a second, it looked as if he had no idea who I was, like he was about to take a bite out of my hand.

Blinking, he came back.

"Sorry," he said, and sat.

"That's what I thought," Capone huffed before popping a squat.

George pretended nothing had happened.

"If you let the Wendigo in," he said, "it seized your stomach and gave you an uncontrollable craving for flesh. The only way to stay alive was to eat another human being. And another. And another . . ." George's eyelids were growing heavy. "How else do you explain all the gnawed bones found around here?"

"What bones?" Capone asked.

"Before this place became a camp, archeologists dug through the area. They discovered bits of ribs covered in teeth marks. Half-skeletons with bones missing." George paused, stifling a yawn. "Maybe, just maybe, there's some truth to the story."

Charles leaned over to me and whispered, "If I was possessed by the Wendigo, I promise I wouldn't eat you."

"Who would you eat?"

"I'd start with Capone. A lot of meat on those bones."

"I'd like to see you try," Capone said.

Charles only stabbed the fire with his stick.

"Me," Capone pontificated. "I'd probably head to the little kids' cabins. Easy pickings. Each bunk is like its own buffet table!"

"Too many little ribs," Thomas said. "They might get caught in your throat."

"How about we don't eat anybody, okay?" George asked, his head listing over to one side. "Anybody else got a good ghost story?"

The cinders hissed before us. The dark pines leaned over our shoulders, breathing down our necks.

Charles shook his head. Mason and Thomas remained still. So did Capone.

I dipped my chin to my chest and focused on my marshmallow. It looked like a bubbling skull. When I glanced back up, I realized everybody's eyes were on me.

"Sorry, guys." I shook my head. "My storytelling days are over."

"But you're so nuts," Capone persisted, "I bet you've got a real whopper."

"I'm out. Officially retired."

"Sure, whatever," Capone huffed. "Chicken."

The oldest trick in the book: *Call a kid chicken and he'll have to prove he's not.*

It wasn't going to work on me.

I wasn't going to give in.

I wasn't.

*But just when I think I'm out, they pull me back in. . . .*

"You want a ghost story?" I asked. "Fine."

I cleared my throat. It had been a while since I'd had a captive audience. I was feeling a little rusty.

"I'm going to tell you about the Tribe."

"Not Spencer's imaginary friends again," Capone moaned.

"Are these the same guys making birdcalls at you today?"

"Weren't they in the cafeteria too?" Thomas asked.

"Laugh it up all you want," I said. "But everybody who hasn't heeded my warning are all dead now, and I'm not, so I'd think twice before making fun of me about them."

"Fine," Capone said. "We're listening."

"There was this middle school," I started. "It was just like every other boring school. Nothing special. Until . . ."

A charred dollop of marshmallow melted off the tip of my stick, dripping against the cinders.

Mason flinched at the hiss. "Until—*what?*"

"There was this one Cro-Magnon kid. Riley was his name. Riley Callahan. Real jerkwad. Used to pick on sixth graders by shoving them in their lockers."

"My kinda guy," Capone said.

"One day, he wandered into the bathroom alone between classes . . . only he never walked out."

"Really?" Charles asked.

"They found his backpack in one of the stalls. All ripped open. Textbooks torn to shreds. But no sign of Riley. Nobody laid eyes on him ever again."

The campfire illuminated every face in an orange glow. They all looked like pumpkins, anxious expressions carved across their faces.

Thomas leaned in. "What happened to him?"

"Nobody knows."

"Boring," Capone mumbled.

"A week later, it happened again. During football practice, this one jock forgot his helmet in the locker room. He went back inside by himself to get it. . . ."

"And . . . ?" Thomas asked.

"Ten minutes go by. Nothing. No sign of him. Twenty minutes later, the coach goes looking for him. All he found was his bloodied football jersey, his number and everything, ripped to pieces."

"Yeah, right." Capone was growing restless. The fire reflected off the metal in his mouth, gooey strings of melted marshmallow caught in the brackets.

"What's the matter, Capone?" I asked. "You afraid?"

"Hardly."

"You should be," I said. "I know your type. Acting tough in front of everybody, while deep down inside, there's a little dribble of pee in your pants."

"Shut up."

"I'm trying to help you, Capone. This is for your own good. Because by the time the third kid disappeared, a pattern slowly started to emerge. These weren't just any students going the way of the dodo—but bullies. Just like you."

"Bullies?" Capone asked. "Like me?"

"All the kids who ever picked on somebody else at school were vanishing. Almost like they were swallowed up by the walls of the school. Only their backpacks were left behind. Not even that, sometimes. Nothing but bits and pieces. Like they'd been eaten alive."

"Good riddance," Charles said under his breath.

"Then everybody started noticing this rank aroma of road-kill in the halls. The custodian realized the decrepit stench was coming from inside a locker. *Several lockers.* Not just anybody's, but the lockers of those bullies who'd disappeared."

I held out my hand, reaching for the invisible locker in front of me.

"So he dialed the combo on one locker and opened it up and . . ."

I paused for a moment, concentrating on dialing the air.

". . . And?" Thomas asked. *"And?"*

I silently opened the imaginary locker door and gasped, eyes widening at the horrifying sight that only I could see spread out before me.

*"Bones,"* I whispered. "A bunch of bones still wearing Riley Callahan's clothes fell out at the custodian's feet. That Cro-Mag's skeleton comes spilling out across the hallway floor, shattering into all its various segments like a game of pick-up sticks. Ribs scattered everywhere. His skull goes rolling over the linoleum. His locker had totally become his coffin. He'd been stuffed into his locker for weeks, left to rot."

"How . . . ?" Charles started. "Who did it?"

I leaned back.

"Turns out there was a tribe of crazy kids, just like you and me—living in the school. They were hiding in the ceiling. During the day, they'd keep out of sight. But at night, after everybody else had left, they'd creep out and roam through the hallways. And now . . . well, now they were getting their revenge against all the students who had ever picked on them before they ran away, one bully at a time."

"He's lying," Capone said, shaking his head. "You really expect us to believe there were kids living inside a school and nobody knew about them? *Impossible.*"

"Fine," I said. "Don't believe me. You wouldn't be the first."

"How come you know so much about them?"

I leaned in closer to the fire. My shadow against the surrounding pines was stretched to colossal proportions.

"Because they asked me if I wanted to join."

Capone hesitated, caught off guard. The rest remained silent, unsure of what to say.

"I would," Charles piped up first.

"Me, too," Mason said.

"You might think twice if I told you how they induct you. . . ."

"How?" Capone asked.

I slowly pulled the sleeve of my T-shirt up to my neck, exposing my shoulder.

Stunned silence.

Mason's eyes widened, and he shrank inside his hoodie.

Everybody—even Capone—stared in disbelief at the pink scar coiling up from the bulb of my shoulder.

The Tribe's very own insignia, singed into my skin.

"No way," Charles said.

"Once you're in, you're a member for life—and there's no going back."

Mason held out his hand, touching the scar tissue with his index finger. His shoulders tensed at the feel of it.

"By the time I realized I was in over my head, it was too late. I had to run away just to survive."

"*No way,*" Charles said again.

"I've been homeschooled for the last six months just so I could keep my head attached to my shoulders."

"So where are your imaginary friends now?" Capone asked.

"Wish I knew," I sighed. "They're out here, somewhere. Waiting for me."

A tree branch snapped behind us—*CRACK!*

We all turned our heads.

Nothing.

Everybody's attention slowly turned back toward the fire.

Nobody said anything.

"They're angry that I skipped out on them, and now they want to make me pay," I said, peering over my shoulder. "They're coming for me."

"*Yeeeeeeargh!*"

A bare-chested boy, streaked in ash, burst through the circle of campers. In his hand, he held a stick used for roasting marshmallows—like a spear.

"*Yeeeeeargh!*"

Two more leapt up behind him and shrieked, their eyes ringed with soot.

Charles squealed and fell over backward.

Capone leaped from his seat, his eyes blasted with panic.

Laughter erupted from the clan of pint-sized cannibals.

It was the Piranhas. The eight of them reveled in their victory, high-fiving each other as they howled loudly.

"Didyouseethelookontheirfacesohmygodthatwasawesomeha hawegotyou!"

"I'm gonna throttle you." Capone rushed for the nearest Piranha, but the kid sprinted back into the shadows. "You better run!"

The remaining Piranhas dispersed in a flurry of limbs and gnashing teeth, sidestepping Capone with every lunge he made. Their cackling continued, drifting off as they ran—Capone close behind.

"Get back here," he yelled, his voice fading.

The rest of us remained by the fire, shaken up. We all looked at each other, unsure of what to do.

Thomas started laughing first, which got Charles to join in.

Before long, we were all laughing at how scared we'd been.

Even me.

It felt like we were all friends.

Almost.

It felt good to be telling a story again.

Not just any story.

*Their* story.

I wish it was just a ghost story. Parts had been embellished for dramatic effect, sure, but not the Tribe. That part was all true.

At least I thought it was.

I peered over my shoulder one last time. Nothing but cicadas grinding away. Nothing but trees.

Nothing but nightmares.

# YOUR REGULARLY SCHEDULED DEPROGRAMMING

tan the Man had been acting funny ever since curfew. I watched him wobble headfirst into the bathroom door after corralling the Middle Kids into the cabin.

"Everything okay, Mr. Man?" I asked him while we all brushed our teeth, watching him doze off on his own two feet in front of the sink.

"Never felt better," he slurred his words, a dollop of toothpaste foam dribbling out from the corner of his mouth, like a rabid camp counselor.

By the time we were all in bed, Stan the Man could hardly hold his head up.

"Lights out, everybody."

With a flick of the switch, we were all plunged into darkness.

"Sleep tight, Spencer," one of my cabinmates whispered. "Wake us if any of your make-believe play pals decide to pay a visit."

That roused a round of snickers.

I curled up into the warm nylon of my sleeping bag. Squinting up at the shadow of Sully's missing flyer, I said, "Wake me up when summer's over."

• • •

Before long, a chorus of discordant snores hacked away at the silence. None louder than Stan the Man, his nasal cavity buzzsawing away by the front door.

*So much for a good night's sleep.*

A new sound rose up from the darkness. It wasn't coming from across the cabin.

If I didn't know better, I'd say it was coming from above me.

". . . Charles?" I whispered.

The sound stopped.

Silence.

"You okay?"

I stared up at the pitch-black above my face.

"I hate this place." Charles's voice slunk out from the darkness. "I hate everybody here."

"Is it really that bad?"

"Every summer, it's the same thing." I could hear the strain in his voice. "Capone picks a fight on the first day, I fight back, we all get in trouble, my mom gets a call from George, she signs off on some new prescription, and I spend the rest of the summer drooling into my breakfast."

There it was again—that sound.

*Was Charles crying?*

"I don't want to lose myself," he sniffled. "I don't want to spend another summer staring at the walls."

"Don't worry," I said, only half-believing the words coming out of my own mouth. "This summer's gonna be a blip. It'll all be over in a month and you'll be back home."

"Home?" He actually laughed. "What's that?"

"We all gotta call someplace home, right?"

"That's a good one," he said. "My mom ships me off to a private academy for the school year. Then she sends me here for the summer. I'm at my parents' house for a few weeks out of the whole year. School holidays and that's it. That's no home."

"Would you two lovebirds shut up, please?" said another camper—Mason, I think. "Some of us are trying to sleep here."

"Shut. *Up.*" Another camper grumbled. "All of you!"

I couldn't fall asleep.

Not completely.

The best I could manage was to pinch my eyes shut and drift off to that space between unsweetened dreams and restlessness, half-conscious and half-dead to the world all at once.

I'm not sure how much time had passed, but somewhere in the midst of my tossing and turning, I had a dream.

I couldn't breathe. It felt like I was drowning, wrapped in a suffocating blackness.

My eyes bolted open. They adjusted to the dark, focusing on Sully's photocopied flyer staring down at me.

She looked different.

As a matter of fact, she looked a lot like . . .

". . . Sporkboy?"

The picture blinked. "Time to tuck you in."

Sporkboy zipped my sleeping bag over my head.

I was swallowed up by black.

"Get me out, get me out, get me out!" I did my best to claw my way out, but my nails were useless against the nylon lining.

There was a sudden tug.

*Thud.*

I landed on the floor and was dragged across the cabin.

*Thud.*

I hit my head on something. Probably the front door.

*Thud.*

I was outside, I think. I could feel the soft earth skidding under my back.

Where was he taking me?

Rock.

*Ouch.*

Root.

*Ouch.*

Pothole.

*Ouch.*

And then—I was levitating.

At least, it felt like I was. No more solid ground below me.

Somehow I was suspended in the air.

• • •

It was impossible to tell what was happening.

*Where's the zipper in this thing?*

I started rocking my body through the air, back and forth. The harder I rocked, the more momentum I gained.

*Just one more heave-ho and—*

*CRACK!*

That sounded like a branch breaking above my head.

I landed hard on my shoulder. Initial impact was on the bulb of my humerus bone, with the rest of me flopping over flat onto the ground.

*That was going to leave a mark.*

A slight shimmer of light reached through a slit in the zipper. I poked my finger through and opened my sleeping bag enough to wriggle out.

I had been dragged out to a pine tree farther off into the woods.

Four sleeping bags had been hung from separate branches. Each one writhed in the air like a cocoon about to burst.

I reached up and tore into the nearest sleeping bag.

Stan the Man slithered to the ground.

"What's going on?" he moaned, half-catatonic. Without his glasses, he looked like a defenseless woodland creature. "What happened?"

He drifted off to sleep again.

"Stan? Mr. Man? You've got to snap out of it. . . ." I grabbed him by the shoulders and shook as hard as I could. "Wake up!"

I leaned into his face until his eyes latched on to mine, then watched them float up into the safety of his skull, leaving only the whites behind. His head lolled over his right shoulder.

"Come on, now—wake up!"

Then it hit me: *Lunch-man-Sporkboy. Black-market meds. Stan had been drugged with our meds.*

George had been dozing off at the bonfire. Stan could barely stand on his own two feet by lights-out.

What if Sporkboy had dosed the counselors with enough valium to put them out of commission for the rest of the night?

I suddenly had a pretty good idea who was cocooned within the other sleeping bags.

If the Tribe had kidnapped the counselors, then what were they planning for the rest of us?

"We've got to get everybody out of here," I said, shaking Stan awake. "*Now.* You need to cut the other counselors down, okay? Before they come back. Can you do that?"

"What . . . are you . . . going to do?"

"Call for help."

As soon as I let him go, he sank to the ground, where he recommenced his buzz-saw snoring.

This is hopeless, I thought. I need to warn the others before it's too late.

I glanced up at the sleeping bags dangling from their

branches, like a livid Christmas tree covered with wriggling decorations.

I'd return for the comatosed counselors.

But first—back to the cabins.

• • •

Ducking into the parking lot, I had a flash of inspiration:

*What if I hot-wired a bus and plowed through camp? Campers could hop on board this yellow bad boy, and I'd press the pedal to the metal and—*

A garden trowel stuck out from the bus's front tire.

*Scratch that plan. Not that I knew how to drive anyhow.*

The only remaining lifelines to the outside world were in George's office.

One telephone. One computer.

One shot.

The path leading to the main cabin was too exposed. Most likely booby-trapped. That meant I was creeping alongside the surrounding tree line, using the cover of pines to make my way to the rear of the cabin and slip through the back.

The window to George's office was open. I peered inside.

*Empty.*

My eyes locked on to the upright microphone sitting on George's desk.

*Now or never, Spence. . . .*

I hoisted myself up and stumbled through the window, then picked myself up and rushed across the room.

Just as I was about to reach the desk, something tripped me.

I hit the hardwood floor. *Hard.*

Wincing, I rolled over and the lights flashed on.

Too much light. I shielded my eyes.

"Peekaboo," someone said.

I lowered my hands.

My eyes adjusted to the brightness.

Compass, Yardstick, and Sporkboy hovered above me.

"Aren't you a sight for sore eyes?" Compass asked, waving his four and three quarters fingers. He had fastened a computer's circuit board to his chest and a rainbow of cables and voltage sources ran down the length of his arms and legs.

To prove his point, Compass punched me—right in the eye.

I rolled over onto my stomach and moaned, cupping the pulp of my brewing shiner. I clamored up to my hands and knees and attempted to crawl, only for a hand to grab my shoulder and flip me onto my back again.

Yardstick sported football shoulder pads, and his legs were wrapped in shin guards. On his feet, he wore cleats that left pinpricks in the floor behind him.

He pinned me in place by pressing his prickly feet against my chest.

"Stay," he said. The spikes burrowed into my skin.

I did as I was told.

"Spencer, Spencer, Spencer . . ."

Somebody was savoring the sound of my name.

I heard the warp of wood just behind my head.

Peashooter waltzed into view. He leaned over me. A bitter chill seeped out from his stare. I would've sworn his irises were made of ice. His baby face had peeled away. He now wore a weathered countenance, his skin coarsened from constant exposure to the outdoors.

It had been six months since I had watched him run off, his face slathered in blood. What was it that he had said to me?

*"This isn't over between you and me. You're dead, Spencer! Dead!"*

How could I forget?

"Miss us?" he asked. "We sure missed you. . . ."

Peashooter had wrapped himself in animal hides. His arms were covered in crow feathers. It almost looked like he had wings. A bleached bird skull was perched on each shoulder, their beaks pointing over his arms.

Branching from behind his head were a pair of deer antlers. A crown of horns.

I could make out the slight scar on the cartilage that linked his nostrils together. The scar I'd given him.

"How did you find me?" I asked.

"Your father's been awfully worried about you. All the trouble you've been causing lately . . . He and I agreed it was high time for an intervention."

"That was you talking to my dad?" I asked. "You were the one who kept calling?"

"He was planning to send you to military school, you know.

Can you imagine? You, Spencer Pendleton, at a *military school*?"

"You wouldn't have lasted a week." Compass sneered. The acne spread along his cheeks and forehead had cratered into jagged pockmarks, like a lunar landscape.

"Somebody had to step in," Peashooter said. "Change your father's mind."

I hesitated, caught off guard. "Coming here was *your* idea?"

Sporkboy held up his hands and shrugged—*Guilty as charged.* Four green Girl Scout sashes were strapped over his shoulders, like bandoliers, crisscrossing at his chest in an *X*.

"Love the new outfits," I said. "Where'd you get them? Headhunters 'R' Us?"

"I'm borrowing them from troop sixty-two," he said. "I'm collecting the whole set. . . . Tonight, I think I'm going to earn my skin-filleting badge."

I noticed their arms were free of Magic-Markered mantras.

"What happened to your tats? Run out of Sharpies?"

"You took our words away, Spencer," Peashooter explained. "When all our markers ran out, our phrases faded away. Now our skin is just . . . skin."

That's when I realized somebody was missing.

"Is Sully here?"

Peashooter pushed Yardstick aside and dug his heel into my Adam's apple.

"Mention her name again and I swear I'll bury you in your sleeping bag where no one will find you."

*A simple "no" would have sufficed.*

Peashooter lifted his foot and started to wander about the office, holding his arms behind his back and puffing his chest out—while I clutched my throat, coughing. He plopped into the swivel chair behind George's desk and leaned back. "I could get used to this," he said, giving himself a spin. "What do you think?"

"Looks good." Sporkboy nodded. "You look good."

"You really think so?"

"It suits you," Compass agreed. "You were born for it."

"What about the counselors?" I coughed, interrupting the love-in. "What're you going to do with them?"

"They can hang out without us for a while," Peashooter said. "Would you feel more comfortable with them? Yardstick here could take you back—"

"If the kids don't phone home," I cut him off, "everybody's going to start worrying. They'll call the camp. And when the counselors don't answer, the next call everybody at home is going to make will be to the—"

"We had a home once," he interrupted. "Until you took it away from us."

"Now we live like animals," Compass said.

"But not anymore." Peashooter flipped the switch on the intercom.

A surge of feedback ricocheted throughout camp.

Bringing the microphone to his mouth, he announced, "Attention, campers! This is your wake-up call. We are sorry to interrupt your regularly scheduled deprogramming, but there has been a change in your summer plans. . . ."

# Part III: Fart of Darkness

*Hello mother, hello father . . .*
*I send you greetings from camp slaughter.*
*Grub is rough here. Flesh is more palatable.*
*I guess that's why this place is called Camp Cannibal!*

# UNDER NEW
# MANAGEMENT

ll campers were woken up and called to the amphitheater. Even the Piranhas were unleashed from their cabin.

Everyone filed in, half-asleep, and took a seat circling the fire pit, probably anticipating some midnight "sharing session" with our counselors. A look of unease was settling over each camper's face as whispers passed through the amphitheater.

I spotted Charles. His eyes widened as he took in my situation—bound to a shower curtain rod before the fire pit. Sporkboy and Yardstick had hefted each end of the rod over a shoulder, like I was a pig on a rotisserie spit.

Compass heaped a pile of kindling into the pit. He lit the fire and the smell of burning pine needles drifted through the air.

"Drop him," Peashooter commanded from the center of the amphitheater. Sporkboy and Yardstick did as they were told, and I landed before the fire—*Ouch.*

Peashooter looked down at me lying there and smiled. The

cold looming within his eyes seemed to lower the temperature whenever I stared at him.

"Ready for this?" he asked me.

"Are you asking if I'm ready for more of your theatrics?"

"You ain't seen nothing yet."

Peashooter's spine went ramrod straight. Chin lifted, eyes wide, he summoned all the fury his throat could muster and howled straight into the air.

"*Oooooooooooooooow!*"

All whispering ceased. The crowd of campers regarded Peashooter with a fidgety apprehension—*Who is this crow-feathered freak?*

Peashooter's arm shot up over his head. Something was in his hand.

Something fuzzy.

It looked like a scraggly blond paintbrush without a handle. It didn't take long for everyone to figure out what it was.

A ponytail.

Peashooter presented the severed clump. "Do I have everyone's attention?"

Nobody said a word.

"Good."

Peashooter tossed George's ponytail into the fire—*Sssssssssss.*

"We are not here to hurt you," he announced. "We are here to help. Your counselors are no longer in control of this camp. They are no longer in control of you."

He paused long enough to let the echo of his words fade.

"*You* are."

The fire behind him crackled as a piece of kindling snapped, sending a flurry of sparks into the air.

"Your parents saw this camp as a tourniquet. A quick fix to stop the bleeding, a temporary solution for what they couldn't be bothered to understand. They would rather throw money at the *problem*, and ship you off to some *program* so that you'd return home to them good as new. They wanted to change you. *Modify* you. How? With pills. With prescriptions. Your parents have manipulated the miracle of modern medicine to bend your brains to their frivolous will. Why? Because *they don't understand you*."

Peashooter stopped and grinned, regarding each camper with the unbridled enthusiasm of a boy about to open his Christmas presents.

"But we do."

Peashooter turned and acknowledged Thomas. I could see Thomas weigh his options: *Should I make a break for it or stay put?*

"If this is how your parents treat you," Peashooter offered him, "if they think you're nothing but a broken toy they can ship off to get fixed—then I say they don't deserve you in the first place. Because, to us—*you're perfect just the way you are*."

The sound of his voice flooded the amphitheater and seeped into the surrounding forest. His words were everywhere.

Inescapable.

Thomas sat upright on his log, his eyes never breaking from Peashooter. His decision was clear—*stay*.

Peashooter pointed to the parking lot where we had been dropped off. "Out there, everyone calls you a *delinquent*. Back at home, your parents call you *emotionally disturbed*."

He looked around to make sure the words were sinking in.

"Well—*this is your new home now.* And your parents will never be invited into *your* house!"

Peashooter looked to Mason. Mason absentmindedly rolled up his sleeves, exposing a rugged terrain of scar tissue that ran the length of his forearms.

"Whatever your mother and fathers are afraid of in you, we want to embrace it," Peashooter said. "We want to nourish that fire within until it scorches the earth!"

Mason nodded. Even from where I was lying, I could see the words landing.

Summer camp was definitely over.

"The first step toward emancipation is to cut ties with those who hold you back," Peashooter pushed on. "Your mothers and fathers, your brothers and sisters, *because they don't deserve to be your family.*"

He paused. "We're your family now."

Peashooter was like the undertow, that invisible force underneath the ocean's surface that pulls hapless swimmers farther and farther away from the shore—until they drown.

I should know. Peashooter had nearly drowned me. I've witnessed the spell he casts over others with nothing more than the power of his words.

Or somebody else's.

"*Disobedience is the true foundation of liberty*," Peashooter recited. "Henry David Thoreau wrote that almost two hundred years ago—and it remains true today. We have liberated you from adult supervision. We have liberated you from the rules of the outside world. The one thing—*the only thing*—we ask for to prove your commitment to our cause is . . ."

"What is it?" Thomas's eagerness betrayed his excitement. "What do you want from us?"

Peashooter turned his head toward me and grinned.

"Him."

# BURN,
## BOYHOOD,
## BURN

**S**o," Peashooter called, "what are we gonna burn first?"

Most kids looked at him as if he'd just spoken to them in Latin, but Mason's eyes widened. He jumped to his feet, unable to control his excitement.

Peashooter stood before Mason, gauging him. "You're the pyro, right?"

Mason dropped his gaze. Peashooter grabbed his chin and lifted his head back up.

"Don't be ashamed," he insisted. "Everybody here has a talent. Yours is the ability to burn. Think of this fire as a symbol for everything that scalds and blisters inside of each and every one of us. Now that it's lit, it will be your responsibility to make sure the flames never die out. Think you're up for it?"

Mason's face brightened. "What can I use for fuel?"

"Anything that burns."

Personally, I didn't think it was such a swell idea to put a pyromaniac in charge of the camp's bonfire, but I figured I would keep my opinions to myself.

Mason hurried out of the amphitheater.

"This fire isn't going to feed itself, people!" Peashooter shouted. "It needs to eat! So I ask you again—*what are we gonna burn first?*"

Mason returned dragging back the banner from the parking lot—TIME TO TURN OVER A NEW LEAF—and before anyone could stop him, he tossed it onto the bonfire. The letters warped and melted into ropy bits of plastic. The air was suddenly suffused with a strong toxic odor as the fire greedily ate through the tarp.

"That's the spirit," Peashooter said. "The rest of you—go to your cabins! Find me fuel! I want a fire so big, it reaches the treetops!"

That's all it took.

Everybody fed the flames, contributing to the conflagration.

Thomas offered up a stack of family photographs. He flicked each pic into the fire, one picture of his parents after another, like he was dealing the flames a hand of dirty poker. The images of his family incinerated in seconds, a royal flush of fire.

Then came a rocking chair. A ratty mattress. Several sleeping bags. Nothing was too small or two large to go in.

Capone tossed George's acoustic guitar in. I heard its six strings snap under the intense heat—*Plink! Plink! Plink!*

*No more crappy sing-alongs for us.*

Several of the Piranhas brought the watercolor portraits they'd been working on in Arts and Crafts.

One brought his suitcase of clothes. He was about to throw the whole thing in when Peashooter asked—"Why torch your clothes, kid?"

"MymomboughtthemIhatekhakishortsIhatebuttonupshirtsI hatethemall!"

"Fair enough."

Peashooter lifted up the Piranha and placed him onto his own shoulders.

"Have at it!"

Like an eight-foot-tall shot-putter, Peashooter spun around in place while the Piranha swung his suitcase over his head before finally letting it go.

*Wham!* Right into the fire.

Peashooter and the Piranha stumbled back, grinning as they watched his suitcase get swallowed by the flames.

Mason slung a sleeping bag over his shoulder as if he were Santa Claus carrying his sack of presents. He upended the bag before the fire, emptying its contents before me.

My books.

Their pages flapped helplessly through the air before hitting the ground.

"Don't!" I shouted.

Peashooter turned at the sound of my voice and nodded. "No books go into the fire," he announced.

"Yeah, but. You said—"

"Nobody burns books, understand?"

"Why not?"

"Because they teach us."

Yardstick used his bulked-up arms to heft an entire file cabinet filled to the hilt with folders. At first, I figured it was going into the fire along with everything else.

"Put it down," Peashooter ordered, pointing to the stretch of ground between me and the pit.

Yardstick dropped it, metal rattling throughout the amphitheater, then returned to his guard position just above me, digging a cleated heel into my hip.

Peashooter grabbed the top compartment's handle and yanked. The drawer shuttled out on its rafters as if it were a human sacrifice he had just disemboweled with his bare hands, exposing all the gory guts of paperwork inside.

"This is what the outside world thinks of you." Peashooter solemnly shook his head as he plucked a single folder out from the drawer and waved it over his head. "This is all that connects you to the old life you had beyond these woods."

Peashooter lobbed the folder high up into the air. Sheets of paper drifted listlessly back down to the ground. Several landed in the fire, where they burned in a blink.

"I want each of you to come here," he commanded. "Take your old self, and make a choice. Keep it—or free yourself forever."

Mason stepped up first. He sifted through the roster of files before plucking out his folder and opening it.

"Out here, you are free to be who you truly are," Peashooter said. "So . . . who *are* you?"

Mason scanned the forms. He shook his head and flung his folder into the flames.

Peashooter pulled a scorched piece of plywood out from the fire and ran his thumb along its charred end. Bringing the dirtied digit up to Mason's face, he rubbed a streak of ash across his forehead.

"From here on," Peashooter said, gripping Mason by the shoulders and grinning, "your name is—*Firefly.*"

Thomas leapt up and raced toward the file cabinet. He found his file and it followed Firefly's into the flames.

"You, we'll call—*Klepto.*"

One by one, the drawer emptied, until the blaze lapped at the stars.

"That's it!" Peashooter raised his hands as if to embrace the flames. His shadow looked like a mutated crow towering above the trees. "Let yourselves go!"

He spotted Charles sitting by himself. "You."

Charles looked behind him, then looked back to Peashooter. "Me?"

"Yes—*you.* Come here."

Charles stood up and stepped before Peashooter, head bowed.

"What's your name?"

"Charles."

"Not any longer," Peashooter said. Rubbing his sooty thumb

across the length of Charles's forehead, he christened him—
"*Jaws.*"

". . . Really?" Charles's face brightened.

"You know what to do."

Charles flipped through the remaining files and chucked his
into the fire. He looked back at me, beaming, as if he thought
I'd be proud.

Can't say that I was.

"You are new men now!" Peashooter wrapped one arm
around Charles's shoulder as he regarded the rest. "All of you!
You are members of the Tribe!"

Compass raised his fist into the air, beckoning the others to
shout along with him—"To the Law of Claw and Fang!"

Thomas joined in—"To the Law of Claw and Fang!"

Mason followed—"To the Law of Claw and Fang!"

Before long, most campers were chanting—"Claw and Fang!
Claw and Fang!"

The only one who wasn't—was Capone.

I spotted him holding back, arms crossed at his chest, observing the rest from the rear of the amphitheater.

Peashooter hadn't noticed. He was too busy talking to
Sporkboy. "Go to the mess hall. Take some rug rats with you.
Grab whatever food you can carry and bring it back."

"Whateverwewant?" one of the Piranhas asked, his eyes
wide with all of the culinary possibilities.

"If you can poke a stick through it and cook it, you can eat it."

The Piranhas all turned to one another and conferred amongst themselves. Finally reaching a whispered agreement, their spokespiranha turned back to Peashooter and asked, "Can we barbecue gummy bears?"

"Sounds tasty to me."

Each Piranha brightened before bolting for the mess hall.

Peashooter turned to the crowd. "Hear that?" he asked, summoning our appetites. "Anything! Hot dogs, marshmallows, ice cream. Tonight, we feast!"

One Piranha fastened a tin cup to the end of a branch and dumped a handful of gelatinous grizzlies inside. Holding the cup over the fire, all those rubbery bears melted into a bubbling molasses. The cup was passed from one Piranha to the next, with each taking a sip of the molten froth. Sufficiently sugared up, each Piranha took off, racing around the amphitheater, gnashing their teeth, spitting out gibberish—

"Gimmemoregimmemoregimmegimmemooooooore."

I watched Firefly fling another suitcase into the fire. The flames embraced its new fuel and bathed his skin in an orange glow. His chest rose and fell as if his heart were trying to kick free from the confines of his rib cage.

Peashooter turned back to me. "You hungry?"

"Not really," I lied.

"Give it a few hours and I'll bet you'll gnaw off your own wrist."

"Beats Sporkboy's cooking."

"Anything you'd like to add to the fire?"

"No, thanks."

"How about . . . *this*?"

He pulled out a folded sheet of paper and slowly opened it in front of my face.

Sully's missing flyer.

"Give that back!"

Yardstick pressed his cleats into my chest. "Stay down."

"Material possessions make a man weak," Peashooter said. "So consider this a gift, from me to you."

Peashooter wadded up the faded flyer with one hand.

"*Don't—*"

He tossed the crumpled ball into the blaze.

"Stings, doesn't it? Having everything you care for taken away from you." He addressed the crowd, pointing at me. "From now on, Spencer's name will be . . . *Rat*."

Several campers laughed, repeating Peashooter's christening. "Rat! Rat! Rat!"

"For the longest time," Peashooter said, "there was no written word in these woods. Rat had taken our library away from us, so we needed to rely on each other."

The antlers attached to Peashooter's head seemed to grow even longer. Their shadow reached for the trees at his back.

"Your counselors told you about the Wendigo," he continued. "They said he was just a ghost story. A myth. But living out here for the last six months, I know he's out there."

"I never took you to be the superstitious type," I said.

A breeze blew through. Pines rustled all around us, and the crow feathers wrapped around Peashooter's arms bristled.

"We're the Wendigos," he said. "These are our woods. That's why we're renaming this place. Camp New Leaf is dead. From now on, our home is called *Camp Cannibal*. Long live *Camp Cannibal!*"

"Long live Camp Cannibal!" the campers shouted back.

"Long live the Law of Claw and Fang!"

"Claw and Fang!"

"Claw and Fang!"

"Claw and Fang!"

There was a scream at the back of the amphitheater. One of the Piranhas shrieked like he'd just seen a Wendigo.

He had.

The towering beast stepped into the firelight.

"Look what I found!" Sporkboy hoisted the moose's head from the mess hall over his own and charged toward the fire, yelling at the top of his lungs.

The glass eyes of Camp New Leaf's placid mascot captured the flames, both black marbles flickering yellow and orange.

When Sporkboy reached the center of the amphitheater, he skidded to a halt and launched the moose's head. *"Bombs away!"*

A cloud of cinders exploded into the air as the flames embraced the decapitated head. Campers cheered.

Peashooter raised his fist and shouted, "Let the wild rumpus begin!"

The Tribe formed a mosh pit around the inferno. Their bodies sweated in the firelight as they belted out made-up songs, slam-dancing before the heaving flames:

*Hello mother, hello father . . .*
*I send you greetings from camp slaughter.*
*Grub is rough here. Flesh is more palatable.*
*I guess that's why this place is called Camp Cannibal!*

I never felt more homesick in all of my life.

Not for a house. Not Mom's or Dad's place. But for a sense of belonging.

I felt homesick for Sully.

It wasn't long before the newly expanded Tribe wasn't singing anymore—but howling like a pack of wolves. Their voices rose into the night's sky and echoed through the woods.

"Ow-ow-*owwwooooooooooo*! Ow-ow-*ooooowwwwooooooooooooooooooo*!"

The moose kept staring up at the stars. The expression on its face never changed as its maple-leafed antlers wilted into the fire.

A flap of its hide slid off the wooden skull and the moose was gone.

I watched as my fellow campers slipped deeper and deeper into savagery. From the glow of the fire, they barely looked human anymore.

# ASTHMA HACK

*really need to get out of here.*

The cord around my wrists was cutting off my circulation, and I could barely feel my fingers as I tugged at my bindings.

Yardstick had slipped off into the mosh pit around the fire. Nobody was keeping an eye on me anymore.

Perfect opportunity to make a break for it.

I wriggled over the ground until the shower curtain rod slid out from between my arms and legs. Bringing my knees up to my chest, I used my bound hands to undo the bungee cord around my ankles.

*Quick, Spencer.*

There was no time to free my hands. Running was priority number one. I leapt onto my feet and bolted for the main path.

*Go!*

*Go!*

*Go!*

I made it about five steps before tripping. With my hands bound and no way to brace my fall, I hit the ground hard. The impact forced the air out of my lungs.

Turning over, I saw Thomas—sorry, Klepto. His foot slid back from the path.

"Ooops," he said.

Before I could catch my breath, Sporkboy flipped me over onto my back and pounced, planting his knees on my chest.

"What's the rush, Rat?"

Even with most of his extra heft burned off his big-boned body, Sporkboy still weighed a ton. He pitched back and forth on his knees like a rocking horse.

A burning sensation started to brew within my lungs. Every bronchiole was suddenly craving air.

"Get off," I strained. I tried pushing him away, but he wouldn't budge.

My fellow campers kept back. None of them said a word. A hush hung over them, some bowing their heads, while Peashooter sauntered up the path toward me.

"I'm no doctor," Peashooter said. "But if I'm not mistaken, I think Rat is showing symptoms of an asthma attack. What do you guys think?"

Compass wandered up next to him. "I read somewhere putting pressure on his chest is about the worse thing you can do."

"You heard the man." Peashooter tapped Sporkboy's shoulder. "Better let him up for air."

"Sure thing." Sporkboy glanced down. "Pardon me."

He crawled off, one knee at a time.

The moment all that excess weight lifted off my ribs, I rolled onto my stomach and coughed.

Where was the air all of a sudden?

I reached for My Little Friend around my neck, but before I could grab it, Compass seized the shoestring and yanked.

My Little Friend scuttled over the ground in front of me.

I reached for my inhaler, my breaths growing shallower. Just as my fingers grazed the plastic canister, Sporkboy kicked it.

My Little Friend skidded even farther out of my grasp.

I had to pick myself up onto my elbows and drag myself across the amphitheater, my breath breaking off into pebbles of staccato gasps.

Charles took a step forward, ready to scoop up my inhaler and hand it to me, but Sporkboy held his hand out. His palm pressed against Charles's chest.

"Stay back," Sporkboy said.

"But—" Charles leaned against Sporkboy's hand, his beartrap jaw flapping open.

"If he needs it so badly, he can get it himself."

The rest of the camp didn't even try to help.

I was on my own with this one.

There were about two feet between me and My Little Friend. Before I could grab it, Compass leaned over and examined it with his cold scientific detachment.

"Is this yours?" he asked.

Without waiting for an answer, Compass punted My Little Friend clear across the amphitheater.

"Don't—"

The trees seemed to uproot themselves and rotate about me. I pinched my eyes shut and reopened them, but the woods kept whirling.

*Round and round and round it goes, where my breath stops, nobody knows. . . .*

I'd had bad attacks before. I just had to remember what to do if I didn't have an inhaler handy:

1. *Relax.*
2. *Keep calm.*
3. *Even your breathing until it's back to normal.*

The O.G. members of the Tribe circled around me as I struggled onto my feet. Behind them, the rest of the camp observed in complicit silence.

I tried breaking through the ring of bodies, but Sporkboy pushed me into Yardstick.

"*Red rover, red rover,*" Sporkboy sang, "*send Spencer right over. . . .*"

Yardstick shoved me into Compass.

The circle tightened as the tendons in my neck started to constrict, clamping down on my windpipe.

"Help . . ." I started.

Compass brought his hand up to his ear. "What was that?"

"Can't . . . breathe."

"You're turning a little blue, Spencer. You should lie down."

My doctor told me it's always better to lean forward. Never lie on my back.

Too late.

Compass rooted his right leg behind my feet and yanked on my arm, sending me spiraling to the ground.

I landed on my tailbone. Totally crushed my coccyx. I was sprawled out on my back. Every pine needle bristling in the trees above my head seemed to simultaneously reach down from their branches and pierce my eyeballs.

Peashooter's head hovered above my own. "You okay, Spence?" he asked. "Need a hand?" He reached out to me, but the weight of my own arm was too much.

The sky was now prickling with yellow spots. I couldn't see.

"Doc . . . tor."

"What's that?" Peashooter asked.

"Get me . . . to . . . a doctor."

"I think he's asking for his daughter," Sporkboy suggested.

"No," Yardstick said. "He's asking for his copy of *Harry Potter*."

"You're both wrong," Compass said, shaking his head. "*Water*. Spencer is asking for *water*."

"Water?" Peashooter scanned the surrounding area. "See any water around here?"

Sporkboy pointed to Lake Wendigo.

"Well," Peashooter said. "If Spencer wants water, let's get him some water!"

The sound of their voices dwindled in my ears.

Hands seized my arms and legs.

The ground was gone.

I was being carried.

Or was I floating on my own?

It felt like I was drifting over the ground, in the air forever. Then I heard the warp of wood beneath me.

The dock. We were on the dock.

I could feel a breeze against my cheeks. It was cold.

Somebody giggled above me. Sporkboy, most likely.

My head rolled to one side and I could see the smooth glass surface of the lake filling my vision.

Nobody tried to stop them. Not one camper.

I wanted my mother.

I wanted my father.

I wanted Sully.

I wanted to breathe.

I wanted to live.

I came to a halt. I felt a wobble in the dock, even though I wasn't touching it.

"On the count of three," someone announced. "One . . ."

I felt myself swing forward.

"Two . . ."

I felt myself swing back.

"Three!"

I swung forward and felt them let go.

I couldn't take a breath before the cold embraced my body.

I couldn't reach the air.

Everything felt heavier, hugging me, pulling me down. The last pocket of oxygen in my chest slipped through my lips, dribbling upwards.

Numbness swept over.

Down, down, down into the dark.

*I can't breathe. . . .*

*I can't . . .*

*I . . .*

A silhouette drifted before me.

The murk made it impossible to make out a face. All I saw was a fuzzy outline gliding effortlessly through the water, a tangle of tentacles obscuring its features.

A hydra-haired mermaid.

# CATCHING UP WITH OLD PALS

I woke on my back. The wooden cage I was in looked like a play-pen for a feral infant. The bars were made of branches, each end tied off with shoelaces or twine.

I was instantly reminded of a quote from *The Call of the Wild*:

*"There he lay for the remainder of the weary night, nursing his wrath and wounded pride. . . . Why were they keeping him pent up in this narrow crate?"*

The sun reached through the surrounding bars. I lifted myself on one elbow. As soon as I boosted my abdomen off the ground, my lungs blazed, setting the rest of my chest on fire.

My lungs felt like they'd been sandpapered.

I could only take short breaths, these pitifully infinitesimal gasps of air. Each rasping grasp at the oxygen sent a shrill whis-tle up from my throat.

I was alive. Just barely—but still alive.

I was already out of breath just from picking myself up, with what little breath I was able to inhale in the first place.

I slumped over. Spent. Good as dead.

There was nothing left in me.

No more fight, no oxygen. Just a shell of inflamed tissue barely held up on a frame of burnt-match bones.

My clothes were still damp. Last thing I remembered, I was plunging into the depths of Lake Wendigo. Everything else is a murky blur of cold water.

*How did I get here?*

A tuft of smoke spirited up from the burned bits of furniture in the fire pit. The moose head had disintegrated. Nothing but the charred tinder sticks of its antlers remained.

The Piranhas were asleep in a heap. They looked like a litter of puppies all piled together, using each other's bodies for warmth. Their chests rose and softly dropped in rhythm, their slight snoring drifting across the amphitheater.

"Look who's still breathing." Peashooter was leaning against a log behind the cage, tossing an apple. "We figured you were done for, up until Yardstick found you on the shore. I'm impressed you could swim all that way on your own."

Had I? There just wasn't any other explanation.

"Welcome to your home-away-from-home-away-from-home." Peashooter drew near the cage until his face was only inches from mine. "Get cozy. You'll be here for a while."

So that was it: I was a prisoner of war.

I remembered photographs of internment camps in world history, where captured soldiers were kept in bamboo cages.

"You . . . win." I wheezed, the bars now between us.

Peashooter laughed. "Say that again."

"Just tell me . . . what you want. . . ."

"You can't quit, Spencer. We've just started!" He took a bite out from his apple. "If all we were after was *winning*, believe me—we would've been running victory laps around you a long time ago."

Peashooter tossed the half-eaten apple directly into the pile of Piranhas. They woke with a start, the apple rolling over the ground—only for the pack to scramble after it, clawing and gnashing at each other until one of them bit down on the piece of fruit. That didn't stop another Piranha from chomping down on the other side.

In seconds, all that was left was the core. It fell to the ground in a puff of dirt.

Peashooter gripped the bars of my cage.

"Who are you, Spencer?" he asked. "Do you even know? You always talk big. But who are you underneath it all? That's who I'm waiting to see." He held out a hand. "Think of yourself as an onion." He balled his hand into a fist. "I'm going to peel away every layer of your existence. Your cocky attitude, that mouth of yours." With each item he listed, he peeled back a finger. "I'm going to strip you down to the very core of your being—and when I reach it, when I reach *the true Spencer Pendleton*, I am going to show you what it feels like to lose everything that matters most. Then—and only then—will you know what it's felt like for us all these months."

"Sounds like fun," I said, rubbing my chest.

"You always valued yourself more than the common good of the Tribe," Peashooter said,

"Only because . . ." I had to take in a deep breath to finish my thought. "Because the common good quickly became tyranny."

*"A rose by any other name . . ."*

". . . would still smell like megalomania to me."

Peashooter flicked a fire ant crawling along his arm.

"I believed in the Tribe," I managed to say. "What it could . . . could have been. But that's not what . . . not what you were using the Tribe for."

"Then help me," Peashooter said, staring straight at me.

"Excuse me?"

Peashooter glanced over his shoulder. "What if I were to give you one last chance?"

"To what?"

"Join us. It's not too late."

I hesitated. "Join the Tribe? *Your* Tribe?"

"Just think of what we could accomplish together! The havoc we'd create!" Peashooter's face brightened. I caught a little glimmer of hope flickering within his eyes. "Everything we need to take a stand is right here!"

A miniscule part of my brain was screaming from the back of my skull—*Yes!*

Then I remembered my pledge to go the straight and narrow. "I can't."

The glimmer in his eyes quickly faded, as though he'd brought a hammer down on a lightbulb. "You're either with us— or against us. You know that, yes?"

"Guess that means I'll be calling this cage home for a while, huh?"

Peashooter stood up and dusted himself off without a word.

"Here," he finally said, almost as an afterthought, as he pulled out My Little Friend from his pocket. My lungs nearly sang—*Hallelujah*.

Peashooter hung the shoestring around the end of a branch directly above my cage. I reached through the bars, but there were three inches between my fingers and my inhaler.

"Better keep breathing," Peashooter said as he started to walk off.

"This beef you've got with me—it's just between us. Why drag everybody else into it to prove your point?"

Peashooter turned to me. "You see me twisting anyone's arm?"

"So you're gonna brand the campers now, like you branded me? Scar them for the rest of their lives?"

"You don't deserve to bear our mark!" The words echoed into the pines. At the sound of his shouting, the Piranhas scurried off, dashing out of the amphitheater.

Before Peashooter could betray his anger any further, he collected himself with a deep breath and recited—"*I went to the woods because I wished to live deliberately, to front only the essential facts of life, and see if I could not learn what it had to teach, and not, when I came to die, discover that I had not lived."*

"Who said that?"

"Thoreau. You really should read him some day."

"My library card got cut to pieces this summer. Long story."

Peashooter only stared. "You have no idea how long I've been waiting for this. Biding my time until you showed up. Now that you're here, the party can start."

"Sure hope Sully got an invite."

The expression on his face curdled. "Your girlfriend won't be saving your ass this time—sorry."

# POSTCARDS FROM THE EDGE

Dear Mom and Dad . . .

Camp is awesome. I'm having the time of my life. I wish I never had to leave. In fact, don't plan on picking me up.

I'm never coming home.

I've made many new friends here, friends for life. They've become my real family now. We've decided to stay here for the rest of our lives.

No hard feelings. Please feed my goldfish for me.

Love, your ex-son . . .

Actually—it wasn't *exactly* like that.

Every cannibal was required to write home to their parents. Even me.

We were each given a postcard with specific instructions: *Write about how much fun you're having. Sound like you mean it.*

No one was allowed to mention the Tribe. No one was allowed to mention the takeover.

Sporkboy was the camp's designated redactor. He was responsible for reading over every postcard before sticking a stamp on it. If he came across any reference to the Tribe, he'd tear up the postcard and tell the camper to start over.

The older campers thought this was a waste of their time. Capone and Klepto had refused to write their cards, so the Piranhas were corralled into the amphitheater, near my cage, and put to work corresponding for the older kids.

A stack of yellowing postcards sat waiting. When the Piranhas were finished scribbling on one postcard, they placed it in the finished pile and took another.

*A correspondence sweatshop.*

The postcards were all the same—a faded photo of Lake Wendigo, taken fifty years ago, with a kid popping a squat in a canoe waving at the camera.

Sporkboy leaned over one Piranha's shoulder, reading what he was writing.

"Start over," he instructed. "Scratch that part out. Start over again. You, too."

"Yougottobekiddingthisisstupidthisisboringwhatarewesup-posedtowrite?"

Sporkboy could hardly muster enough patience to finish a thought. "Just write something like—*I miss you guys. Wish you were here*. That kind of crap."

"Ifyouknowwhatwearesupposedtowritethenwhydontyou writeitforusthen?"

"Fine. Fine." Sporkboy jotted down his own postcard. "Just copy that, okay?"

> I can't wait to see you guys at Parents' Day. I'm counting down the days until you come up here and I get to show you how much personal progress I've made. You guys are in for a big surprise. . . .

Somebody had to make sure the Piranhas didn't burn the camp down. Their blood sugar was at an all-time high. Whatever they could put in their mouths, they'd gnaw right through—paintbrushes, crayons, pencils. They might have lost a few digits by the end of the summer if somebody didn't keep them occupied.

From the looks on their faces, the Piranhas hadn't taken a bath in days. Their cheeks were smudged with dirt. Pine needles had tangled in their hair.

One of the rabid pack spotted a frog hopping across a

mossy log. He picked it up and cupped it with both hands. "LookatwhatIvegot!"

The others circled, eager to see. "Lemmehaveit!"

"Quititgetbackhesmine!"

"IsawhimfirstIsawhimfirst!"

Almost at once, the other Piranhas began to yank at the boy's arms. They pulled and pried at his hands, but he wouldn't let go.

The boy snapped his teeth.

"Hesmineminemine!"

The Piranha holding the frog lost his grip. The amphibian leapt to the ground and tried to retreat up the main path.

But Sporkboy brought his foot down.

*SQUISH!*

The Piranhas froze. Collective tears welled up in their eyes at the sight of the green intestines dangling from Sporkboy's heel—but brimming behind their heartbreak, I could see rage.

"Youkilledhimyoukilledhimyoukilledhim!"

The Piranhas swarmed with such ferocious speed, all eight sets of legs collectively charging at Sporkboy, you would have thought they were one very hungry, very perturbed beast.

"Stay back." Sporkboy rolled over a log and started crawling along the ground on his belly. "Get away, I'm warning you!"

The *clack-clack* of the Piranhas' gnashing teeth grew louder.

"Don't do it," I spoke up.

The Piranhas snapped their heads toward me and tilted their necks.

"Sure you could rip him to pieces," I reasoned. "But what would that accomplish?"

"Nothing," Sporkboy whimpered. "Absolutely nothing!"

"Hewouldbedead," one particularly ticked-off Piranha said.

"Kill him and then the rest of the camp has to come and kill a couple of you guys, and then you have to retaliate by killing a few more of them, and on and on . . ."

"Soundslikefunfunfunfun." The Piranhas all gnashed their teeth.

"I'm not saying Sporkboy doesn't deserve it. But think of it this way: Martin Luther King Jr. once said, 'Nonviolence is directed against forces of evil rather than against persons who happen to be doing the evil.'"

All eight collectively cricked their heads to one shoulder.

"What he's saying is, you should seek to defeat the true source of evil—we're talking Evil with a capital *E* here—not just somebody who's been victimized by Evil themselves. And just look at Sporkboy. He's a pawn in somebody else's master plan. Does he really strike you as someone who's perpetuating a capital *E* kind of Evil?"

The Piranhas mulled this over before stepping away from Sporkboy, muttering under their collective breath—

"Hegotluckywewouldhaveeatenhimalivetherewouldbenothingleftbutbones."

The pack burst into eight separate campers and ran off.

Sporkboy rose, dusting himself off. "Thanks. I think."

"Don't worry about it," I said. "Been a while, hasn't it?"

"Peashooter says I'm not supposed to get all friendly with the prisoners."

"You don't actually do *everything* Peashooter tells you to do, do you? I mean, you and me used to be pals. . . ."

"He said you'd say something like that."

There had been a time when Sporkboy feared being called everything from Lard Bucket to Garbage Disposal to Barf Bag. But this new Sporkboy didn't seem to think about what anybody else called him.

In fact, he didn't think at all. Peashooter had that covered.

"What else did Peashooter say about me?"

"He said you'd try to convince me to let you out."

I acted like I was offended. "He actually said that?"

Sporkboy nodded. "Peashooter said you'd try to undermine his authority by saying how we used to be friends and that you'd say anything to get me to doubt what he says because you're a . . . a . . . a *submersive influence*."

"I guess there's no pulling one over on you, is there?"

"Peashooter says I'm supposed to . . ."

"Okay, okay—I get it," I cut him off. "Whatever Peashooter says, goes."

Sporkboy kicked his heel through the dirt.

"Just following orders," he mumbled. He looked over his

shoulder. When he saw the coast was clear, he turned back to me and whispered, "There is this one little *eensie-weensie* favor I wanted to ask you, though. . . ."

This was my chance.

"Name it."

Sporkboy's face brightened. "Really?"

"Just between you and me."

He clapped. "I stole this book on Greek mythology from the younger kid's cabin. It was a picture book, but whatever—the drawings were pretty cool. My favorite part was the chapter on Scorpio killing Orion. Do you know the story?"

"Scorpio . . . ?"

"Yeah! Orion was this loudmouth who couldn't keep his trap shut, so Artemis sends this ginormous scorpion down to fight him, and guess who gets stung to death? Now they've both got their own constellations in the sky. . . ."

"I'm not really hearing the favor part of your request here."

Sporkboy grinned. I caught a glint of the ol' craziness flickering at the back of his eyes. "I was wondering if, you know, you wouldn't mind a little reenactment."

"I don't know, Sporky," I backpedaled a bit. A lot. "I'm a Libra. I wouldn't even know how to play Scorpio."

"Don't worry about that," he said. "I've already found somebody."

• • •

"Time to plaaaaaaay . . . *The Dangling Death!*"

Klepto and Capone, along with a few other cannibals from camp, entered the amphitheater, lured in by Sporkboy's game-show-host impression.

How does one play *The Dangling Death*, you ask?

The rules are simple:

1. *Sporkboy catches an animal. Preferably one with pincers. Or fangs.*
2. *Sporkboy ties its tail to a string.*
3. *Sporkboy dangles the animal from a tree branch and slowly lowers it into my cage until it bites/stings/claws me and I die a most painful death.*

Sporkboy had tied his string around the crustaceous torso of a scorpion.

There are around fourteen hundred different subspecies of scorpions in this world. Only twenty-five of them are known to carry venom capable of killing a human being.

I really didn't feel like pressing my luck and finding out how venomous this particular scorpion was.

"Place your bets, boys," he said. "How long until the Rat gets it?"

The cannibals circled around my cage.

"I got a buck on him getting stung in less than a minute," Capone said.

"Two bucks on thirty seconds," Klepto said back.

"You're on!"

"All bets are in," Sporkboy said. "Time to play!"

I crouched as far down into my cage as I could, hoping to avoid my descending houseguest. Its claws retracted back and sprung open, ready to snap.

"Everybody keep your eye on the claws," Sporkboy proclaimed as if he was a sports announcer. "All eyes on the claws!"

The cheers grew as more campers entered the amphitheater. Before long, a dozen cannibals had surrounded my cage, all rooting for my opponent.

*"Scorpio! Scorpio! Scorpio!"*

I spotted Charles pushing through the crowd. As soon as he forced his way up front and saw what was happening, he pleaded, "Quit it, guys! You can't do this!"

Capone shoved him and he fell to the ground.

"Go play somewhere else, beaver-teeth."

Charles scrambled back to his feet and rushed out.

"Scorpio's going in for the kill!" Sporkboy cried.

My back was pressed against the cage. I inched to one side, only for the scorpion to spin toward me on its string and snap at the air.

*"Scorpio! Scorpio! Scorpio!"*

Only inches remained between us.

*Four inches . . .*

The scorpion's claws had me cornered.

*Three inches . . .*

Its tail stabbed the air just before my nose.

*Two . . .*

Yardstick raced into the amphitheater with Charles following behind. He plowed through the crowd and grabbed the string.

Just in time.

The scorpion halted, its tail missing its intended target by millimeters.

"Hey!" Sporkboy yelled. "That's mine!"

Yardstick spat back, "Want to explain to Peashooter how our prisoner died on your watch?"

I cringed underneath the scorpion as its tail kept jabbing at the air, so close to my nose.

"You're no fun," Sporkboy muttered, straining.

Yardstick yanked the string hard and Sporkboy lost his grip. The scorpion flew from my cage high above everyone's head.

I leaned my head back. We all did, watching it ascend, claws clasping at the air—only to freeze mid-flight, before beginning its descent back to planet earth.

Towards me.

My cage.

My face.

My early grave.

"Watch out, watch out, watch out," Klepto yelled and jumped back. "It's coming in for a landing!"

Everyone scampered to avoid the free-falling scorpion.

Capone pushed Charles out of his way as he rushed up the main path.

All I could do was press against the side of my cage in hopes that it didn't crash through the lid.

*Here it comes.* . . .

*Here it comes.* . . .

*Here it* . . .

I lost sight of the scorpion. One second, it was only a few yards away from the ground. The next, it just—*vanished.*

Sporkboy had craned his neck along with everyone else, toward the sky. When he looked back at the rest of us, we all saw the scorpion sprawled across the front of his face.

From between its claws, I could see Sporkboy's wide-open eyes.

"Huh—huh—*help.*"

The scorpion had perched its hind legs on Sporkboy's quivering bottom lip and reeled back its tail, ready to sting him on his forehead.

"Swat it off!" I shouted.

Sporkboy batted the scorpion away with one sweep of his arm, but not before the forward-curved stinger jabbed him— *twice*—above the radius muscle, delivering its venomous payload.

I could sense the collective wince from everyone—chests locked, breaths held, muscles tensed.

Sporkboy glanced down at his arm as if he'd never noticed he had one before, then looked up to the rest of us.

"I'm feeling a little woozy, guys. . . ."

Sporkboy's eyes fluttered up into his skull, and he belly-flopped to the ground.

"What do we do?" Yardstick panicked.

"Somebody's got to suck the poison out," I said.

Everyone stood stock-still.

"*Now*," I insisted. "He doesn't have much time!"

"No way." Klepto shook his head. "I'm not doing it."

"Somebody's got to!"

"Count me out," Capone muttered.

"Just drag him over here," I said. "I'll do it."

Nobody moved.

"Yardstick!"

He snapped out of it and turned to me.

"Drag him over!"

Yardstick lugged Sporkboy toward my cage.

Sporkboy's head rolled over his shoulders. His arm was already ballooning up from an allergic reaction to the poison. I grabbed his wrist and flossed his arm through the bars. A droplet of yellow venom seeped out from each sting wound.

*Sure hope this works. . . .*

Leaning over, I wrapped my lips around Sporkboy's arm and began sucking.

An acidic liquid rushed over my tongue. I spat it out, half-expecting it to sizzle when it hit the ground.

I leaned in and leeched the venom from the second wound.

"What do we do now?" Yardstick asked.

"Take him to the infirmary. There's bound to be some sort of anti-venom first-aid kit. Compass should know."

Sporkboy turned to me and woozily smiled, his freckled cheeks swallowing his eyes. "Just like old times, huh?"

"Yeah," I said, out of breath. "We should do this again."

I could still taste the venom in my mouth, burning at the back of my throat.

*I really have to get out of here.*

Yardstick hoisted Sporkboy up by his arms. "You saved his life."

"Hee woodve wone wuh wame fo mee." I managed to maneuver my mealy mouth to enunciate the words, my tongue nearly numb from scorpion poison.

"No." Yardstick shook his head. "He wouldn't."

"Yooo pwobawbwee wight."

# ALWAYS NAP WITH ONE EYE OPEN

ood afternoon, cannibals." Peashooter's voice boomed from the PA system. "Homesickness is weakness leaving the body. For anyone feeling homesick, know this—it passes. Like a bad cold. And once it's gone, you will realize that this is your home now. With us."

George's cabin must have become the Tribe's central command. Whenever Peashooter wanted to address his minions, all he had to do was flip the switch.

*Let the brainwashing begin. . . .*

"Everyone meet in the amphitheater in five minutes."

# ABANDON ALL HOPE YE WHO CAMP HERE

The banner hung from the pines for all to see as they entered the amphitheater.

Cannibals were greeted by the sight of a timber skeleton towering up from the fire pit, its wooden bones ready to be ignited.

Firefly had been dragging every loose bit of lumber from around camp that he could find. A mess hall table. Chairs. A wooden canoe.

Even our suitcases.

"Hey," Charles cried. "That's mine! And those are my clothes in it!"

"You heard Peashooter's orders," Firefly said as he emptied a rusted can of gasoline onto the kindling wicker man. "Anything that burns."

Peashooter promenaded in wearing George's whistle around his neck.

I noticed each of the original Tribesmen had their own lanyard now. They must have yanked them off the counselors.

*He who wears the whistle possesses the power.*

Nobody had seen George or the others since the takeover. Were the counselors still strung up in the woods? Rumors spread that they were all at the bottom of Lake Wendigo. Or chopped up and fed to the Piranhas for breakfast.

"Firefly," Peashooter said. "I have a gift for you."

Peashooter presented a box of strike-anywhere matches to Firefly.

Firefly shook the tiny box next to his ear. The thin wooden rattle seemed to soothe him. An eerie calm washed over as he pulled out a match and struck it against the flint.

A flame blossomed only inches away from his face. He inhaled the bouquet of sulfur through his nose.

Klepto piped up. "Maybe you should step back—"

Too late. Firefly flicked the match into the timber skeleton's rib cage.

*WHOOSH!*

Firefly was knocked to the ground by the fireball. Klepto rushed over and picked up his smoldering comrade.

"Your eyebrows! They're . . ." Klepto glared at Firefly's face. "*Gone.*"

Sure enough, where Firefly's eyebrows had been was nothing more than singed skin.

"Who needs eyebrows?" Firefly just shrugged before rushing out of the amphitheater. He nearly ran into Yardstick carrying a scarecrow tucked under his arm, the dummy sporting a New Leaf T-shirt with the maple-leafed moose head. He had made a whole scare-family from the looks of it, hefting five more into the amphitheater, all stuffed with straw from the archery range's hay bales.

Capone took one look and guffawed. "Who're they supposed to be? Our counselors?"

Yardstick strung up his scarecrows from the tree branches extending over the amphitheater. Peashooter stood next to one holding a quarterstaff made from a sawed-off broom handle.

"We must protect our home," he said as Sporkboy—still looking a little puffy from his scorpion sting—distributed quarterstaffs. "We begin today with some simple drills from

*The Merry Adventures of Robin Hood.* Any of you read it?"

No one responded.

Peashooter had his work cut out for him. He patiently inhaled through his nose, then recited—*"Robin Hood hid in Sherwood Forest for the next year, during which he gathered around him many other outcasts. . . . Sherwood became a refuge for those who had been wronged or were on the run . . . They vowed to treat their oppressors as they had been treated."*

"I liked the movie better," Capone muttered, elbowing Klepto in his ribs. Klepto snickered.

Peashooter thrust the end of the quarterstaff into the scarecrow's chest and the grin faded from Klepto's lips.

"Stand with your left foot forward and your right foot back," Peashooter instructed. "Keep your right foot turned outward at ninety degrees."

The cannibals did their best to mirror Peashooter's battle stance.

"On my mark, thrust. One, two, three—*strike!*"

Klepto's jabbing was a little off-center due to his eye.

"Again!"

Klepto recalibrated his aim and hit his target directly in the heart.

"Again!"

Capone lunged forward and took the head off of his scarecrow. *"Hiyaw!"* Loose bits of straw puffed out from the perforation and scattered across the ground.

"Again!" Peashooter called out. "Feel the fog lift from your minds! You can think for yourselves now! You are alive once more!"

"When's lunch break?" Capone asked, killing the mood almost immediately.

Peashooter turned to him, unimpressed. "When you get your drills down."

"Is that when the fun's supposed to start?"

"This isn't about fun. This is about protecting what's ours."

"Then why don't I go protect the mess hall?"

"If you don't like it," Peashooter said, "you can join the counselors."

Capone kept his eyes locked on Peashooter, but he stayed quiet.

*The natives are getting restless. . . .*

The Piranhas weren't allowed weapons of their own, so they went after their scarecrows with their bare hands.

Firefly returned, rolling a hay bale into the amphitheater's entrance. He struck a match and tapped the straw with its flame, then let it ride.

"Fire in the hole!"

Several cannibals had to leap out of the way as the burning bale bowled down the amphitheater's walkway and crashed head-on into the bonfire.

*WHOOSH!*

A flurry of sparks burst through the air, like a blizzard of orange snow, the stray cinders sprinkling upon our poor scarecounselors. Before long, their straw bodies started to smolder.

Thin wisps of smoke rose up from their shoulders.

"The fire's spreading," Yardstick shouted as he rushed to control it.

Too late. Flames erupted from their heads, like they had dyed their hair a sweltering yellow. Before long, their entire bodies were consumed by flame. The heat from the fire was so intense, I could feel it reaching for me through my cage.

Yardstick took his quarterstaff and knocked one down, sending the burning scarecounselor to the ground. Several cannibals circled around and beat the flames out with their own staffs, laughing as they went.

Capone knocked another burning straw man from its branch. "Home run!"

Before long, all the campers had joined in, beating the blaze out.

Let me go on record as saying I really didn't think it was wise to give a group of emotionally disturbed teenagers their own weapons.

But that was just me.

Not that I was complaining. It had been over twenty-four hours since I had taken my last Chlorofornil tablet. No fog for as far as my mind's eye could see.

Just clear cerebral skies.

While, all around me, I couldn't help but hear the neurological time bomb ticking within everybody's chemically imbalanced brain, now going cold turkey.

Detonation in T-minus a few days of detoxing.

*Three . . .*

*Two . . .*

*One . . .*

• • •

Night fell fast. Everyone had shuffled off to their cabins for some shut-eye, exhausted from an endless day of "training."

The camp remained quiet. I had the amphitheater all to myself, alone in my cage, so I watched the bonfire continue to lick the air. I could almost make out the shapes of our personal belongings still in the blaze—the back of a chair, a scrap of a photograph poking out from the surrounding ashes, a melted toothbrush.

Sleep wasn't coming for me anytime soon.

I flipped onto my back and stared up at the pines swaying overhead. Their branches rocked back and forth, and I couldn't help but think of the first time I saw Sully. How her hair hid her face, protecting her from the world just on the other side.

Footsteps.

Someone was walking into the amphitheater. It was dark, but the silhouette had to be at least six feet tall.

Yardstick.

The dim glow from the fire illuminated the athletic pads strapped to his shoulders, making him look like a life-size action figure.

"Time for another cleat crunch?" I asked.

Yardstick only shook his head.

"Then what do you want?"

Yardstick slipped his hand through the cage. It took me a few blinks to focus on the pile in his palm.

Berries. Bulbous and ink-stain black.

I pinched one between my fingers. "Poisonous?"

"See for yourself."

I popped the berry in my mouth and bit down. A sour jolt coursed through the rest of my body.

I cupped the berries in my hand and downed them all at once.

The tart tang tasted good.

No—not just good. *Phenomenal.* An entire day had slipped by since I'd eaten anything. I had no idea how hungry I actually was.

"You need to get your energy back," he said. "You can find them throughout the woods. Stay away from any red berries, though. Those are the poisonous kind."

"Are you breaking me out?"

"Not yet."

"So what are you doing here?"

"Keeping you alive."

I hesitated. "No offense—but I'm having a hard time believing the word of somebody who tried aerating my chest with his soccer cleats."

"You're just going to have to trust me."

"Can you at least give me a weapon? Something to defend myself with?"

Yardstick nodded. He reached into his back pocket and slipped something through the bars.

I took it from him. There were no sharp edges. No blades. No trigger.

Just soft pages.

A paperback.

"This isn't exactly what I had in mind. . . ."

"It might not be the kind of weapon you want, but it's the one you'll need."

He sounded like a fortune cookie.

"So I'll just paper-cut anybody who comes at me?"

I brought the cover up to my face, straining to read the title in the dark.

*Animal Farm.* Written by . . .

George Somebody.

"Got anything I can read with?"

Yardstick tossed me a penlight. "Don't let anyone catch you with that."

"I'll take it under advisement," I said. "Why are you helping me? I'm pretty sure associating with known defectors could get you in trouble."

"I promised a mutual friend."

"Sully?"

Yardstick didn't answer.

"What happened to her?"

"She just disappeared. Nobody knows why. Peashooter told us. He said she . . ."

The words evaporated before he could give them sound.

"What . . . ?" I asked. "Died?"

Yardstick nodded.

"You believe him?"

"No way." He shook his head. "Peashooter's not the same. He's worse. Much worse. The longer he's been alone out here in the woods, the more he blames you."

"For what?"

"*Everything.* Sully didn't want to have anything to do with his master plan if it meant hurting you. She and Peashooter would always argue over it. And then, one day—*poof.* She was gone. We'd only been out here for a little while, right after we'd left Greenfield, and Sully just vanished. That's when Peashooter really lost it. He made us swear allegiance to him. Threatened to hang us from the trees by our feet for the bears to eat. Compass and Sporkboy swore right then and there, while I—I just couldn't make sense of it anymore." He went quiet for a moment, shaking his head. "This isn't why I joined the Tribe. This isn't the Tribe I joined."

A low rumble ruptured the air. Yardstick cricked his neck back and examined the night sky.

No stars. Nothing but thunderheads.

A thought popped into my head. "Remember when you used to be so shy, back at school? You could barely look me in the eye. What happened to that guy?"

"A lot can change in six months," he said. "Especially out here."

Yardstick froze.

"Someone's coming. Hide the book."

Yardstick disappeared just as quickly as he had arrived.

*Where am I supposed to hide a book?* I scrambled to find a spot in the cage that could keep the paperback concealed. Easier said than done.

I could bury the book in my armpit.

I could stuff it down my shirt.

Too late. Whoever was coming, I could hear the soft shuffling of their feet just at the top of the amphitheater.

I opted to sit on it, stuffing the book under my rump.

Somebody cleared his throat. I looked up to find Charles standing at the amphitheater's entrance. His lips lifted up into a smile, then lowered. "Hey . . ."

"Hey."

"Who were you talking to?"

"Just me, myself, and I."

"Oh." He slowly shuffled his way up to the front of my cage.

"So what should I call you now?"

"Jaws," he said, poking out his chin. "Not bad, huh? Don't worry. I'll ask Peashooter if he can give you a better nickname than Rat."

*Yeah, like Dead Meat.*

"I'll stick with my real name, thanks."

He seemed perplexed by this. "But Peashooter says, out here, away from home, we're all free to be whoever we want to be."

"I'd rather just be who I am if that's all right."

"Whatever floats your boat."

*Rocks your boat is more like it.*

Charles burrowed his heel into the dirt, waiting for me to say something.

"Do you really feel like these guys are your friends?" I asked.

Charles mulled it over before nodding. "Peashooter accepts me for who I am."

"And who's that?"

Silence. Charles pinched his eyebrows. "Thought you might be hungry, so I brought you these."

He held up a handful of marshmallows. "They got a little sticky, sorry."

"How about helping me break out?"

Charles buried his chin into his chest. "I can't."

"Sure you can." I wrapped my hands around the bars. "All you've got to do is unlock the lid and . . ."

"They'll skin me alive."

I pressed my forehead against a bar. "Friends don't let friends die in cages."

"I should be going."

"Charles, wait."

"It's *Jaws*." The vehemence in his voice surprised me.

Charles dropped the wet wad of marshmallows at my feet. He turned and shuffled back up the path without saying another word.

• • •

The grumble in my tummy muted itself after I scarfed down the white puffs. The marshmallows expanded within my stomach like I had inflatable intestines.

*Time for a little bedtime tale. . . .*

I ran my thumb over the pages of the paperback, feeling the breeze against my skin. I cupped the penlight in my hands and leaned in until the words were only inches away from my face.

Somebody had circled sentences. Phrases were underlined. Passages boxed in with pencil. Whoever had read this book before me did a good job of annotating it.

The story was about a group of rebellious animals who take over their farm from their human owner. At first, all animals are treated as equals—until one group, the pigs, become "more equal" than the others.

Before long, their hierarchy is just as bad as that of the humans they ousted.

Thunder rolled over my head. Louder this time.

Closer.

The first drops of rain started to fall, wetting the pages of the paperback. Plump bulbs of water burst across my skin as I stuffed the book under my shirt.

The rain intensified, pouring down thick and steady, pounding my back.

My first bath in days.

# ASHES TO ASHES

Peashooter stood before the wet embers of the bonfire.

Very quietly.

Firefly shifted his weight from one foot to the next, waiting for him to say something. *Anything.* But Peashooter refused to acknowledge his existence.

The rest sat on their logs and watched Peashooter's fists continuously clench and release as he stared at the soggy black paste at his feet.

"What happened to my fire?" he asked.

This was a parenting ploy I was pretty familiar with—*I'm not mad at you . . . I'm just disappointed.*

But I wouldn't put it past Peashooter to pop his top at any moment. I must admit, the confines of my cage were feeling pretty cozy right about then. This was the first time I was thankful to have a set of bars between him and me.

Peashooter finally turned away from the fire pit and faced Firefly.

"Your orders were pretty clear, weren't they?"

"Well, yeah—"

"What were they again?"

"*Never let the fire die out.*" Firefly's voice wilted under the intensity of Peashooter's glare.

"*Exactly.* One very simple order."

"But . . ."

"*But?*" Peashooter leaned into Firefly's face. "But—*what?*"

"It . . . rained."

"Should I get somebody else to take care of my fire?"

"No!" Firefly cried. "I can do it. I swear."

Peashooter addressed the rest. "Some of you have taken advantage of the Tribe's kindness. Haven't we given you your freedom? A place to call home? All the food you could ever eat? All we've asked for in return is allegiance—your devotion to our cause. That means preparation. *Training.* We need to take care of our home."

"You mean housekeeping?" Capone muttered.

Peashooter shook his head. "Parents' Day is only a couple days away. We need to be ready to welcome your families with open arms."

"What're you going to do?" I asked. "Imprison our parents?"

Peashooter grinned.

"You can't be serious."

"Why not? Isn't that what they've done to you all of these years? I think it's high time we turned the tables on Mom and Dad. . . . Wouldn't you agree, cannibals?"

The roar of approval from the rest of the campers made me shrink back.

"He's crazy," I tried to implore to the others. "You all know that, right?"

"*We're all mad here,*" Peashooter quoted *Alice in Wonderland*. "*I'm mad. You're mad. . . . You must be . . . Or, you wouldn't have come here.* Isn't that right, boys?"

The Tribe cheered even louder this time.

"Don't worry, Rat," Peashooter said. "We've got a very special surprise in store for your mom and dad."

I gripped on to the cage and shook the bars. "If you touch them, I swear I'll—"

"You'll what? What could you possibly do to me?"

"I'll . . . I'll . . ." I had nothing. I felt completely flustered. "Why are you so bent on making everybody else's mom and dad pay for something they haven't done?"

"They've done plenty."

"To you?"

"To all of us. Parents are the same, no matter who their children are. Now, everybody—*up on your feet!*"

Newly galvanized, the cannibals formed a line before Peashooter. Only Capone grumbled, but nobody paid him any attention.

Today's military drill: marching.

"On my command," Peashooter called out. "For-ward, march!"

His ragtag battalion of cannibals shifted their weight onto their right foot while stepping forward a full thirty inches on their left.

"Right, left, right, left, right!"

Keeping their eyes focused up front, the column marched through the amphitheater. The leg of the cannibal behind moved at the exact same time as the corresponding leg of the camper up front.

"Right, left, right, left, right!"

Sporkboy had dragged in an aluminum trash can from the mess hall. Flipping it over, he pounded out a cadence with a pair of wooden spoons.

Peashooter chanted as if he were a drill instructor—

*"Mom and Dad sent me away,*
*They never loved me anyway.*

*They dropped me off at summer camp,*
*Now I sleep in the cold and damp.*

*They don't care if I'm dead or 'live,*
*That's okay, I joined the Tribe!"*

I watched them march for what felt like hours. Seeing them circle around my cage all morning made me light-headed.

"Sound off," Peashooter barked.

"One, two," the Tribe called back.

"Sound off!"

"Three, four!"

"Halt!" Peashooter commanded.

The processional of cannibals came to a complete halt.

"About-face!"

The column spun on its heels, now standing upright, shoulder to shoulder with one another, facing their pleased leader. He walked down the line.

"By the time summer is over," Peashooter continued, "you will all be lean, mean, head-hunting machines. You will all have something to be proud of. You will have a sense of self-worth. Of pride. Of belonging to something bigger and better than yourself! You will be a part of this family we call the Tribe!"

Peashooter stopped before Charles. "Chin up," he instructed.

Charles lifted his chin accordingly.

"Let me hear your war cry," he instructed.

"*Yaaaaaargh!*"

"You expect to scare anyone with a cry like that? Louder this time!"

Charles's neck cricked to the side. "*Yeeeaaaaaargh!*"

"Louder!"

"*Yeeeeeeeeeeeaaaaaaaaaargh!*"

"Would any of you be afraid of a battle cry like that?" Peashooter asked the rest of his regiment.

"No!" they promptly responded.

"Hear that?" Peashooter shouted directly into Charles's ear. Charles couldn't help but wince. "You couldn't even frighten the rug rats if you tried! Now drop to the ground and give me twenty!"

Charles plopped onto his belly and struggled through his push-ups. Peashooter placed his foot on the small of his back and leaned in, adding his heft.

"Put your back into it," he shouted.

"I . . . can't."

"You can't—or you won't?"

*"Can't."*

Peashooter pressed his foot down until Charles dropped face-first into the dirt. "Stay down until I say you can get up! The rest of you—double-time, march!"

Still pinning Charles to the ground, Peashooter looked to Firefly. "That fire isn't going to light itself, is it?"

"On it." Firefly didn't hesitate, quickly patting down his pockets.

His eyes widened.

Something was missing. I could tell from the panic eclipsing his features.

"Where are my matches?" He kept searching his pockets on his hoodie, digging and re-digging—but nothing.

He spun around in circles, scanning the ground.

Nothing at his feet.

"Who took them?" He lifted his head, searching through the amphitheater, until his eyes locked onto Klepto. Up came an accusing finger. "You!"

Klepto looked over his shoulder, then back at Firely. "Who? Me?"

"You stole them, didn't you?"

Klepto shrugged. "What're you talking about?"

"You did," Firefly shouted. "I know you did!"

"Now hold on a sec—"

Klepto took a step back, only for a tiny blue-and-red cardboard box to fall at his feet. He picked it up quickly, but the rattle of wooden matchsticks broadcast Klepto's guilt.

"Give them back!" Firefly let out a howl as he bolted up the amphitheater's path and rammed his shoulder directly into Klepto's stomach.

The two of them blurred into a flurry of fists. Their bodies knotted into one another, rolling over the ground.

Capone laughed, starting to chant—*"Fight! Fight! Fight!"*

Peashooter wasn't pleased with the outbreak. *"Stop!* Stop this at once!"

But nobody listened. Instead, more cannibals joined in— *"Fight! Fight! Fight!"*

Peashooter motioned to Yardstick, who dutifully marched over and gripped Firefly by the back of his sweatshirt. With a single yank, Yardstick pulled Firefly off of Klepto—only Klepto wouldn't let go, accidentally ripping Firefly's hoodie in half.

*"Fight! Fight! Fi—"*

Firefly stumbled forward, his torso exposed.

From his neck to his navel, he looked like a crudely fashioned doll made from a massive stash of Silly Putty.

*Burn scars.*

We had all known about Firefly's burns. But none of us had seen the full extent of them. His hoodie had hidden the vast expanse of mottled tissue from us, as if his sweatshirt had been his true skin all along.

Firefly's face flushed into a deep beet red while his chest marbled up in a strange mixture of pink and white.

"Stop looking at me!"

Firefly grabbed the tatters of his sweatshirt and pressed them to his chest, then forced his way out of the amphitheater, pushing through his frozen comrades.

The Tribe stood there, silent. Unable to move.

None were more aghast than Peashooter.

• • •

"Everybody, just . . ." Peashooter started to say before chasing after Firefly. "Just mind your own business."

A hush hung over our heads. Nobody could make eye contact with one another, unsure of what to even say after what we had all just witnessed.

"This is for the birds," Capone muttered as he shuffled off. Several others followed behind him.

Yardstick made sure everyone else had left before sneaking over to my cage with a canteen of water.

"What's going on here?" I asked between greedy gulps. "Did you see that?"

Yardstick slipped a paperback through the bars. "Hide this, fast."

"Another weapon?"

"Read it the right way and it might be," Yardstick said over his shoulder, making a hasty exit. "Don't let Peashooter catch you with it."

"Wait—"

Too late. Yardstick was gone, abandoning me with the book. *Walden and Other Writings* by Henry David Thoreau.

Never read that one before.

Opening it, I found a note written in the margins:

> *Being a prisoner doesn't have to make you weak. It can make you stronger, as long as you stick to your ideals. What will you stand up for?*
>
> *The She-Wolf*

• • •

I had to wait until nightfall before bringing the book back out, having risked paper-cutting my butt by tucking it into the waistline of my shorts just next to my copy of *Animal Farm* for the last five hours.

I was building up a library just under my behind. Nobody would ever think to look for a book down there.

*Or want to.*

I had hidden my penlight alongside the lower crosspiece of the cage. Clicking it on for a walk through *Walden*, I spotted an underlined passage in one of the other writings:

> *Read the best books first, or you may not have*
> *a chance to read them at all.*

I better get cracking.

• • •

Thoreau had spent two years, two months, and two days in the wilderness and chose jail over supporting a war he didn't believe in—which, at the present moment, was something I could personally identify with.

In the margins, The She-Wolf had written:

*Think Mandela. Think Gandhi. Think King. They were all prisoners at some point—but they never let the bars get in the way.*

I might not be able to muscle out from my cage, but maybe I didn't need to.

*You can break my body, Peashooter, but you won't break my mind. You can't touch my spirit. My will to live is stronger than any cage you can cram me in—*

Someone was in the trees.

Two somebodies. They had been perched right over my head. I caught a glimpse of their silhouettes just as they leapt from one branch to the next.

I hadn't even noticed. How long had they been up there, looking down at me?

"Come back!"

A face slowly emerged from the shadows.

A girl.

But not like any girl I'd ever seen. She was older. Her cheeks were streaked with a series of red and blue stripes. Her blond hair had been braided into a pair of Celtic-looking knots around the sides of her head. She wore a New Leaf T-shirt like the rest of us, but the shoulders appeared to have been lined with white feathers.

*Were those wings?*

"Who are you?" I asked. "Some kind of swan maiden?"

"What do you think?" Her no-nonsense attitude threw me.

"Are you . . . the She-Wolf?"

That made her laugh. "No cigar, kid."

"But you're from the girls' camp, aren't you?"

"What gave me away?"

"So you guys are spying on me now?"

"In your dreams." She turned toward the woods, about to disappear into the shadows once more.

"Wait—please!"

She stopped, impatiently looking my way.

"Take me with you."

"Sorry, kid." She shook her head. "No boys allowed."

The swaying pines seemed to wrap their limbs around her agile body as she bounded from one branch to another on the neighboring tree, whisking her away.

"Happy reading," her voice trailed out from the darkness.

# OUR BOOKS HAVE BECOME BATTLEFIELDS

The sun rose up from the tree line.

Dawn was upon us. A new day would be here before long—and with it, the next step in Peashooter's master plan for global takeover.

Peashooter had requested the Piranhas' presence in the amphitheater for a little Farts and Crafts—while I, crammed in my cage, had to listen to his diatribing. He slid a bowl of water into my pen, like I was his dog and he my benevolent master.

Peashooter posed as the Piranhas painted portraits of their fearless leader.

Peashooter wearing a general's uniform festooned with a chest of medals, head held high.

Peashooter standing valiantly atop a heap of counselors.

Peashooter crossing the Delaware River.

One Piranha worked on a portrait of Peashooter completely

comprised of gummy bears, but he got hungry halfway through and ate his leader's likeness.

*Must've been a starving artist.*

"Gather round," Peashooter instructed the kiddie cannibals. "You are the next generation of the Tribe, our future, so I want you to take what I'm saying to heart."

Their young Piranha minds were soft putty in Peashooter's hands.

"Who knows? Maybe one day, you might start a tribe of your own."

"Franchising tribes already?" I jabbed from the confines of my cage. "Next thing you know you'll have your own chain going. Would you like that tribe super-sized, sir? Your total comes to $3.57. Drive around to the next window, please."

Peashooter put on his best poker face and acted like he hadn't heard me. "You need to know where you all came from. Time for a lesson in Tribal History."

"Emphasis on *HIS*-story."

Peashooter turned to me and glared. He wasn't about to let me steal his thunder. "See him?" He pointed. "Why do you think we keep him in a cage?"

"Becauseheatesomebody," one Piranha offered.

"I've been boxed up in here long enough that I probably *could* eat somebody," I said. I spotted a few smirks.

"That's what happens when you betray your Tribe," Peashooter shot me down. "Rat is an enemy of all his kind."

"That's from *White Fang*," I said. "As a matter of fact, you strike me as something of a Lip-lip character yourself, Peashooter."

The Piranhas looked puzzled. "Whatisa*liplip*?" Their spokes-piranha asked.

"Lip-lip is a dog in *White Fang*," I said before Peashooter could pipe up.

"He was the leader of their pack," he cut in.

"For a while," I cut back. "He knows White Fang is a threat. So he bullies him in front of all the other dogs. He even gets them to torture him. But what Lip-lip doesn't know is that his hounding only makes White Fang stronger. It's his bullying that transforms White Fang from a little puppy into a fierce dog."

Peashooter sensed I was up to something. "Just because you perused a few chapters doesn't make you an expert. Try living in the wild, like we have."

"Hear that?" I nodded to the Piranhas. "Peashooter thinks crashing in the counselors' cabin is roughing it."

"I've been roughing it out here a lot longer than you. . . ."

"What nature programs do you watch on the TV in George's room when everybody else has fallen asleep?"

The Piranhas gave each other a perplexed side-glance.

"There's no television in George's . . ."

"Do they get cable all the way out here?" I asked.

"Nobody's watching any TV!"

"Next thing you know, Peashooter will be saying there's no more chocodogs or gummy bears—because he's saving them all for himself."

"That's not true," he first said to me, then turned to the Piranhas. *"Not true."*

"How's the food supply holding up, Sweet Pea?"

"None of your business."

The Piranhas volleyed their attention between us. Nobody had openly opposed Peashooter's authority before. This had to be more fun than history.

"I'm not asking for myself, personally," I said. "I was more looking out for the interests of the Future Cannibals of America here."

"Why don't you put a cork in it, Rat?"

"I'm sorry." I cupped my hand around my ear. "I couldn't hear you over all the grumbling stomachs."

"Shut up." Peashooter stumbled with his most unimaginative retort yet.

"I'd be careful if I were you, kids," I said to the Piranhas. "Won't be long before the older campers start eating you little ones."

The cluster of kids started gnashing their teeth. "Notifweeat themfirstnotifweeatthemfirstnotifweeatthemfirst!"

"Remember," I said. "You are what you eat—so steer clear of Capone, okay?"

*"Enough,"* Peashooter shouted. "Nobody is eating anybody. You are all equals in the eyes of the Tribe."

"Is that so?" I asked.

"It most certainly is," he snapped back without a second's hesitation.

This was my chance.

I cleared my throat and lobbed *Animal Farm* straight in his face.

*"No one believes more firmly . . . that all* campers *are equal."*

Peashooter's eyes slowly opened wider.

I kept reciting—*"He would be only happy to let you make your decisions for yourselves."*

Peashooter's mouth cracked open as the words sunk in, his jaw drifting down to his chest.

I didn't let up—*"But sometimes you might make the wrong decisions, comrades, and then where should we be?"*

Peashooter looked as if I had yanked his reading list out from underneath him. I took advantage of his shock and deciphered. "Peashooter says he treats you as his equals, but has he really given you back your power? Or is he calling the shots?"

The Piranhas turned their attention to Peashooter, waiting to see how he would react.

"There's no way . . ." he started to say, but the words died in his mouth. He started up again. "There's no way you could've read *Animal Farm.*"

"George Orwell's great," I said. "He knew that when a man turns into a tyrant, the first thing he destroys is his own freedom."

Peashooter closed in on my cage. "Don't lecture me about Orwell."

"Frightening, isn't it?" I asked the Piranhas. "It's always the people who are so ignorant that have so much influence."

The Piranhas collectively winced. Together, they all took a sharp breath through their gritted teeth—*Oh, snap!*

Peashooter reached his arm through the bars, but I leaned back before he could grab me.

"You don't think I've read it like a hundred times?" The expression on his face knotted as he threw a quote from *Animal Farm* back at me: *"Bravery is not enough . . . Loyalty and obedience are more important . . . Discipline, comrades, iron discipline!"*

Peashooter didn't waste any time following it up: "Translation—Loyalty to your Tribe is what matters most, no matter what this *subversive element* says."

I lobbed another quote back at him: *". . . this was not what they had aimed at when they had set themselves years ago to work for the overthrow . . ."*

"Don't listen to him!" Peashooter blurted. "He's trying to undermine the Tribe's authority with a . . . with a book!"

"And Peashooter's trying to brainwash you!"

Peashooter's eyes darted around the amphitheater as he desperately searched his memory for another Orwellian retort.

Nothing came.

He grabbed hold of the bars on my cage and gave them a good shake, his face inches away from mine.

"You think you can beat me, Rat?"

"I think you're losing control of your new recruits, and that scares you. I think you're in over your head, and I know you know I'm right. I think things are going to get pretty hairy around here, and I for one don't want to see what happens next."

Peashooter wiped his face clean of any emotion.

Without betraying a single sentiment, he unlocked my cage.

He flipped the lid open and stepped away.

"Then leave."

Peashooter held out his hand as if to offer the woods up to me.

"Go."

I slowly stood up. My spine sang a song of relief as I stretched. My back was aching from countless hours of crouching.

I was free. Actually free.

"But before you run away," Peashooter said. "I've got one last question—*where are you going to go?*"

"As far away from here as possible. See you around."

Peashooter only shook his head. "The sad truth is, you've got nowhere to go. No home, no school. No friends. You've got no one."

"Nice try," I said. "My mom'll take me back."

"Really? You mean your mom who you lied to so many times that she stuck you with your deadbeat dad? *That* mom?"

"You don't know anything about her."

"That's interesting, because when the two of us talked on the phone the other day, she said she felt like she couldn't protect you from yourself anymore."

My knees softened.

"Not from us," Peashooter said. "Not from the outside world. She can't protect you from yourself. *You, Spencer.*"

"You're lying."

"Am I?"

My mind drifted. I couldn't think of a comeback quick enough. "I'll go back to my dad's, then."

"How many times did you break out from his house? Ten? Twenty times? You really think he'll take you back?" He recited—*"Our houses are such unwieldy property that we are often imprisoned rather than housed by them."*

I took a deep breath and grabbed hold of the cage, ready to hoist myself out.

My wrists locked.

Freedom was in my grasp. All I had to do was lift one leg over the side of the cage and then the other.

All I had to do was walk through these woods.

Just cut through that vast, desolate stretch of trees and then . . .

And then what?

"What's wrong?" Peashooter asked. "Can't think of anywhere to go?"

The Piranhas kept looking back and forth, waiting to see what I would do next. They were egging me on with their eyes—

*Runrunrunrunrunrunrunrunrunrunrrrrruuuuuuuuuuuuun.*

"Admit it, Spence," Peashooter said. "We're the only family you have left. You're one of us and you always will be, no matter how hard you fight it."

Before I knew what was happening, I was slowly sinking back into the confines of my cage.

The bars lifted over my head, and Peashooter locked the lid, sealing me in.

"Welcome home, *Rat*," Peashooter said.

I brought my legs up to my chest and held myself back from crying.

Peashooter was right.

This was the closet thing to a home I had now.

# WILLIAM
## SHOW-AND-TELL

**G**ood morning, cannibals," Peashooter's voice rumbled through the PA system, dragging me out from my sleep. "Today, we'll be reading from *White Fang. . . .*"

The sky was still gray. It must have been early. The sun barely reached through the surrounding woods. Dew dampened my clothes.

*What day is it? What time?*

Time had lost its shape. I felt I'd been caged for weeks. The only way to determine the days passing were the morning announcements, where Peashooter read from the Tribal Required Reading List:

*"The aim of life was meat,"* he recited. *"Life itself was meat. Life lived on life. There were the eaters and the eaten. The law was: EAT OR BE EATEN."*

I hadn't eaten for what felt like months. Weakness was

seeping into my bones. All I could do was sit and bake in the sun, growing more disoriented.

A silhouette outside my cage shifted before me, moving closer. "Who's there?" I rasped. "Who are you?"

I blinked, but I couldn't focus. The fuzzy form took a step forward.

I couldn't believe it. Air escaped my lungs with a croak.

"Dad . . . ?"

I rubbed my eyes and squinted.

"Dad—is that you?"

"Spencer?" His voice was thick, distant, as if my ears were wrapped in cotton.

I could feel my heartbeat quicken. "Dad, please—you've got to help me."

"You could've stopped this," he said. "All you had to do was run away with your li'l head-hunting friends when you first had the chance. You really would've done me and your mom a huge favor. I don't know how she put up with you for so long. . . ."

"At least she tried." I lost it. "That's a lot more than you can say!"

"Admit it." Dad rubbed a hoof over his ear. "All those times you broke house arrest were just half-assed attempts at getting my attention, weren't they? That's why you always got caught. You wanted to get caught, so I'd take you back."

"What are you saying?"

"Are you gonna eat that grass?"

"... Dad?"

That's when I noticed he had a set of antlers.

"Do you mind if I take a nibble?"

A six-point buck had wandered up to my cage. It had a tawny brown body with white patches speckling its haunches. It stared back at me, chewing.

I had been talking to a deer.

"Sorry about the outburst earlier. . . . I really haven't been myself lately."

The buck's ears fanned backward. He abruptly spun his head around, sensing someone coming our way. He bounded off into the woods with a series of quick leaps.

"Send help," I called out after him.

Compass came down the path carrying a plastic honey-bear bottle tied to a string. "Who're you talking to?" he asked.

"Nobody you know."

Compass fastened the honey bear from a branch just over my cage with its head pointed down, golden fluid welling up within the bear's see-through skull.

"Breakfast's served," Compass said as he popped the container's cap.

Amber ooze sluggishly seeped out from the spout. I craned my neck until my head was positioned underneath the flow and opened my mouth.

*Wait for it . . .*

*Wait . . .*

*Wait . . .*

The first dollop of honey hit my nose. I'd been off by an inch.

I corrected my receiving position.

Honey landed on my tongue and rolled down. Its sweetness spread throughout my mouth. *Finally*—my first meal in what felt like forever.

"Thanks," I said in between swallows. "You're all right, Compass. Really."

Compass waited for me to swallow. "That's very sweet of you to say. I'm sure it has nothing to do with the fact that you're stuck in a cage right now."

"I know we've never really seen eye to . . ." I started, suddenly forgetting the rest of my sentence. "Eye to . . ."

My eyelids started to feel heavy.

Dizziness washed over.

Compass started talking. "Peashooter should've gotten rid of you when he had the chance." The sound of his voice dropped several octaves. "I told him to, but he wouldn't listen to me. He likes you too much—and that makes him weak."

"He suuuure has a funny way of showing it," I said, my words slurring.

"The truth is," Compass said, "if Peashooter had his way, you would join us once and for all. But if you became a member of the Tribe, before long, you'd be Peashooter's second-in-command. And where would I be?"

His acne undulated in fluctuating color.

"I feeeeel funny," I said, and shook my head.

"Sweet dreams, Rat," Compass said before his head became a pimple-ridden balloon and floated off his shoulders.

The honey continued to dribble down my face. I was too sleepy to duck the flow, trapped like a prehistoric insect as it slowly becomes fossilized in amber. Archeologists would excavate my perfectly preserved remains centuries from now.

I'd be the discovery of a lifetime: a petrified cave-camper.

• • •

I had the strangest dream. My skin was crawling away. It felt so unbelievably real. Even in my sleep I would've sworn my flesh was marching right off my bones.

*Wait a minute . . .*

My flesh was on fire. Hundreds of pinpricks were scattering along my arms and legs.

I opened my eyes and discovered I was covered in ants. They nibbled on the film of honey I was glazed in. I tried swatting them off, but they simply skittered across my hands. I could feel them scrambling across my scalp and down my shirt.

"*Ah!*" I yelled. One had crawled into my ear.

When Compass had said *breakfast's served*, he wasn't talking about my meal.

He was talking about *me*.

I was a human picnic.

A splash of water snapped me out of my panic.

Compass stood in front of my cage with a bucket. He splashed me again, extinguishing the ants crawling across my body. Who knows how many hundreds of times I'd been bitten.

Compass leaned over my cage and examined me. The Rorschach test of his acne had changed since the last time I saw him.

"Check out that sunburn," Compass exclaimed. "You're as red as a lobster!"

That's when I noticed his pinkie.

Fastened to the end of Compass's missing fingertip was the metal spike of a drafting compass. He had disassembled the two halves at the hinge, throwing away the pencil fastener and keeping the needle.

"What are you going to do with that?" I had to ask.

"Make a point," he said as he waved the spike perilously close to my left eye.

Klepto entered the amphitheater behind Compass. "Coast is clear."

Compass popped the lock with his pinkie and flipped the lid open. "Get out."

"If it's okay with you," I said. "I'd rather just stay in here. . . ."

They each grabbed an arm and yanked me out from the cage. My feet scraped the ground as they dragged me away, leaving two trails of overturned dirt in my wake.

"Where are you taking me?"

"Archery range," Compass said. "Peashooter gave Klepto a

copy of *Robin Hood*, and he ate it up and now he wants to be an archer."

Klepto nodded, reciting from the book—"*. . . I could put this arrow clear through that proud heart of yours before a friar could say 'grace.'*"

"Only problem is," Compass continued, "when it comes to target practice, there's not a lot of variety."

The camp had transformed itself over the last few days, now overrun with propaganda from some kind of despotic presidential campaign. I spotted posters of Peashooter's countenance hanging from the trunks of trees. Quotes from his favorite books had been graffitied across the cabin walls.

The Tribe's stick figure had been spray-painted across each cabin door, its spear raised over its head. Wrapped around the emblem in bleeding letters, it read:

# LONG LIVE CAMP CANNIBAL! LONG LIVE THE TRIBE!

"Love what you guys have done with the place," I said.

Compass pushed me toward the archery range. "Just keep moving."

I was shoved before a hay bale, my back pressed against the target sheet. Klepto tied my hands together. "For your safety," he said.

He shook a can of spray paint—*clack clack clack*—and spritzed a series of black rings across my T-shirt. Black tendrils of paint dribbled down my shorts.

"Hold still," Compass instructed. He polished a red apple on his shirt and took a bite before perching it on top of my head.

All my bones had turned to jelly by the time Klepto and Compass had situated themselves behind the firing line.

Klepto slipped an arrow into his bow and pinched his good eye shut. It looked as if his lazy eye was staring off somewhere behind me.

A tremor rushed up my spine that sent the apple rolling off my head.

"Um—guys?" I called out across the field. "The apple fell."

"That's okay," Klepto shouted. "I wasn't aiming for the apple!"

"*Whoa, whoa, whoa!* Hold on a sec. I was under the distinct impression Peashooter wanted to keep me alive."

"Guess we'll just have to tell Peashooter it was an accident."

My knees buckled underneath me.

"Help!" I shouted. "Anyone! Help!"

Compass ran over and picked up the apple at my feet by stabbing it with his compass-pinkie. He stuffed the partially eaten piece of fruit into my mouth.

"*Ssh.*" He pressed his compass-pinkie to his lips. "Keep quiet so Klepto can concentrate."

Compass rejoined Klepto behind the firing line and shouted, "Show them how we shoot in Sherwood!"

Klepto resumed his firing stance. He slipped the arrow between his fingers and pulled back on the bow's string.

My teeth sank deeper into the apple's skin. The hinges in my jaw started to ache. Juice dribbled down my chin.

"Ready," Compass instructed.

I closed my eyes.

"Aim . . ."

Apple juice was pooling up at the back of my throat. I almost choked.

"*Fire!*"

I heard a swift *swish* as the arrow buried itself into the hay bale at my left.

"I thought you said you were a pro at this," Compass said. "You were way off!"

"That was a warm-up," Klepto insisted.

I spat out the apple. "Guys—don't do this."

"Ready," Compass intoned.

Klepto slid a second arrow in between his fingers.

"Aim . . ."

Klepto pinched his good eye. His lazy eye drifted up toward the sky.

I closed mine as tightly as I could—and in that darkness, I felt a quote from Martin Luther King Jr. surge up from my throat. I had no choice but to release it:

"*The non-violent resistor not only avoids external, physical violence,*" I shouted, "*but he avoids internal violence of spirit. He not only refuses to shoot his opponent, but he refuses to hate him!"*

Desperate times call for desperate measures. And I was just about as desperate as they come.

"Nice try, Rat," Compass called out. *"Fire!"*

I had less than a second for all thirteen years of my life to come flashing before me—birth, elementary school, holidays, vacations with Mom and Dad, middle school, joining the Tribe, my first kiss with Sully, getting kicked out of the Tribe, coming to camp—and now, my execution.

*Um . . . Why am I not dead yet?*

I slowly cracked one eye open.

Yardstick was standing between me and Klepto's empty bow. He had pulled off one of his athletic shoulder pads and was holding it in front of my face.

The arrow had lodged itself within the padding—the tip of the arrowhead poking through.

I nearly wet myself.

"Have you gone mental?" Compass whined. "Klepto could've killed you!"

Yardstick took a moment to collect himself. "Peashooter will kill you both if he finds out you took the prisoner from his cage."

Compass stared at Yardstick. "You've been awfully protective of the Rat lately."

"Your point?"

"Seems like you're looking out for him."

"I'm looking out for *you*," Yardstick shot back.

Compass took a few steps closer, getting right into Yardstick's face. "Sporkboy told me how you busted up his fun the other day."

"Did he also mention Spencer saved his life?"

"He must've skipped that part."

"Well, he did. Sporkboy would be fertilizing this field if it weren't for him."

"You can't keep an eye on the Rat all the time. If I were you, I'd try keeping an eye on myself for a change."

Yardstick didn't flinch.

Klepto broke the silence. "If you're so worried about him, you put him back."

"Fine by me." With a simple heave-ho, Yardstick lifted me off the ground and laid me over the length of his shoulders.

"Thank you, thank you, thank you," I whispered as he hefted me away.

"Nobody should be treated that way. I don't care whose tribe you're in."

The sun had begun to set by the time Yardstick returned me to the amphitheater. He unlatched the lid on my cage and flipped it open.

"*Please*—don't put me back in there."

"I have to." He plunked me into the cage before dropping the lid back down over my head.

"Don't leave," I pleaded. "I can't spend one more night stuck in this cage."

"It's not time yet." Yardstick pulled out a wadded napkin from his pocket and slipped it through the bars. "Eat this. It's not much, but it's something. I had to wait until everybody else ate and pick up whatever scraps were left."

I opened up the napkin and found a few yellowed pebbles. They looked like the droppings of some animal who'd eaten a lot of corn.

"What's that?"

"Tempeh, maybe? I don't know. . . . Sporkboy ran out of hot dogs, so Peashooter's implemented a ration."

I took a bite. The brittle soybean turd crumbled apart in my mouth. "So much for eating whatever you want, whenever you want."

Yardstick swapped my copy of *Animal Farm* with another book through the bars when nobody was looking.

*The Call of the Wild.*

"I've already read this one."

"You should re-read it."

"Says who?"

"A mutual friend," he whispered, then left.

• • •

Night was now here. The low glow of the bonfire pulsed just a few feet away. Firefly had pulled the beds out from the cabins, abandoning the mattresses and breaking down their frames.

When there were no more beds, he went back for the mattresses.

And when there were no more mattresses, he burned all the tables in the mess hall. Then all the canoes and their paddles.

After our suitcases and our clothes were gone, he pried the shutters from the cabin windows and unscrewed the front door from cabin three.

I was alone. Utterly alone.

Pulling out the penlight and clicking it on, I came upon an underlined section in the book: *The dominant primordial beast was strong in Buck, and under the fierce conditions of trail life it grew and grew. Yet it was a secret growth. His newborn cunning gave him poise and control.*

The light started to flicker and fade.

The batteries were dying.

*Great. Now I can't even read.*

I swatted my palm against the penlight in hopes of rejiggering a little battery juice, but the intensity of the beam only dimmed.

The fading light struck the front row of logs in the amphitheater.

Something seized my attention.

I had to squint, but just on the other side of my cage, in the front row, I spotted a tiny heart carved into the log. I'd seen that carving before. A spear pierced through the superior vena cava. The spearhead poked out from the etched muscle's bottom chamber, a single droplet of blood dribbling off the tip.

Stretching across the left ventricle, it read:

SULLY.

Across the right:

SPENCE.

Just before the batteries died completely, I saw wrapped around the whole heart the word:

FOREVER.

# CLASS
## IS IN
### SESSION

**C**amp Cannibal received one heck of a wake-up call this morning.

A camp-wide chorus of ear-piercing shrieks peeled through the woods.

*What the heck is going on out there?*

Sporkboy stumbled into the amphitheater wearing nothing but his boxers. Several leaves clung to his skin. He frantically scratched at his chest as he raced by.

*"Aaaaaargh . . ."*

Sporkboy tripped on a log and took a header, tumbling toward the fire pit. He skidded face-first across the ground before grinding to a halt in front of my cage. He lifted his head up and found me staring. "What's happening to meeeeeeee . . . ?"

I got a good look-see at the leaves wallpapering his body. Each was divided into three separate almond-shaped leaflets.

How does that rhyme go again?

*Leaves of three, leave them be!*

Red splotches of swollen skin had cropped up along his upper chest and neck. All along his arms. His face. He moaned low as he picked himself up and bolted out of the amphitheater, scratching at his chest as he went. His voice reverberated the farther he ran down the path, quickly cutting itself off with a splash.

Compass was next, pink patches of poisonous oil stains scattered all over his arms and legs. He raced through the amphitheater, a poison sumac leaf clinging to his forehead.

"*Make it stop, make it stop, make it stop.*" Compass clawed at his skin as he rushed for the soothing waters of Lake Wendigo.

Peashooter stormed into the amphitheater in his boxers, the tri-cornered imprint of poison ivy sprawled across his chest.

"I don't know how," he seethed. "But I know this was you. You're gonna eat ivy until you choke!"

The word *choke* echoed through the trees.

Somebody had tucked the Tribe in with a blanket of itch-inducing ivy. I couldn't help but grin, the warmth of the sun spreading over my face.

• • •

Cannibals groggily filed into the amphitheater and took their place along the logs, greeted by a tribe of pink ghosts. Capone nearly buckled over at the sight, doing his best impression of a donkey having an epileptic fit—"*Heehawheehawheehaw!*"

Truth be told, it was hard not to laugh at the sight of Peashooter, Compass, Sporkboy—even Yardstick—completely slathered in calamine lotion, head to toe.

Just looking at each of them, I could read the thoughts racing through their minds—*Whatever you do, just don't scratch, don't scratch, don't scratch.*

Yardstick busied himself by hanging a new banner over my cage. It read:

## CLAW AND FANG 101

He glanced down at me—and winked. I suddenly realized that tricky son of a gun sure seemed a lot less itchy than the rest, even if he was painted pink.

"Pretty crafty payback," I whispered. "Was it you?"

"Nope," he uttered in a low tone. "And I'm not taking the fall for it, either."

Professor Peashooter emptied his lungs into George's whistle as he paced before the simmering fire pit. His skin was caked in dried calamine. When his muscles tensed, the coating cracked, sending a flurry of pink flakes to the ground.

"Listen up," he announced. "We will bring last night's culprit to justice. Until then, we must—"

"Seems pretty clear to everybody here that it was him," a

Pepto-complexioned Compass said, pointing at me. "So let's string him up already!"

"And how exactly did I do all this?" I leaned back against the bars of my cage. "I hate to state the obvious here, but I've been indisposed these last couple of days."

Sporkboy had been frantically scratching at his belly with both hands. Pink streaks of his fingernails raked over the slope of his torso. He paused long enough to point at Klepto. "I saw him wandering around the archery range yesterday. There's a whole bunch of poison ivy back there. He could've done it!"

"Whoa, whoa . . ." Klepto held his hands up. "I didn't do it."

"That's what you said about stealing Firefly's matches," Sporkboy chimed in.

Hearing his name, Firefly stood at attention and shouted— "Keep the bonfire burning at all times!"

"I swear it wasn't!" Klepto backed up, making sure no one was behind him.

"He's lying," Sporkboy insisted. "I can just tell. Look at him!"

"It was the Rat," Compass said. "He's the root of all our problems."

"Blame me all you want, Compass," I answered back. "But if you ask me, it sure sounds like you guys are having a hard time managing your own membership."

"Enough," Peashooter said—while, simmering at the back of his gray eyes, his thoughts were obvious: *Don't scratch, don't scratch, don't scratch, don't scratch.*

"If you can't keep your own house in order, Peashooter, how can you—?"

"*Enough!*" Peashooter shouted, silencing all cross-talk. "We cannot let some *subversive element* impede our plans. We must continue with our training—"

"More marching in circles?" Capone had heard enough. "Count me out."

"It's time we educated ourselves. You'll be instructed by our tribal faculty."

Peashooter nodded to Compass. "Science, chemistry, and explosives."

He pointed to Yardstick. "Engineering and weapon assemblage."

To Sporkboy. "Home Ec."

"You guys are our teachers now?" Capone asked. "School's out!"

"Class is *always* in session."

"Is this supposed to be summer school or summer camp?

A wave of dissent washed over the amphitheater.

Tides were turning, I could tell.

Just in time.

"Look at what the Tribe has done for you." Peashooter was having a difficult time maintaining his composure. "Haven't you been able to do whatever you want out here? To eat what you want?"

"What food?" Capone asked. "There isn't anything left!"

The Piranhas gnashed their teeth at the air—

"Nofoodwhatarewegonnaeatnowwearestarvingwhatarewe gonnaeat?"

"We've got no food," Capone continued. "We don't have anywhere to sleep because Mr. Pyro over there burned all of our beds. . . ."

Firefly flung a pillow onto the fire, stoking its meager flames. "Gotta feed the flames! Gotta feed the flames!"

"We're hungry," Capone kept going. "We're cold . . ."

"And we're *homesick*," Charles said out of the blue.

The word spread amongst the Piranhas, drifting from one mouth to the next—"Homesickhomesickhomesickhomesickhome sickhomesick."

Peashooter wasn't hearing it. "Food is easy to find. But what about your freedom? Who gave that back to you? I did! You're in charge of yourselves for once and for all—thanks to me!"

"Only Peashooter's a little bit more in charge than the rest of you," I piped up.

Capone turned to face me in my cage. "What's that supposed to mean?"

"It's from a book."

"Great." Capone rolled his eyes. "*Another* book."

"Don't listen to him," Peashooter shouted. "He's trying to confuse you."

"Remember George and his little poop therapy sessions?" I asked the crowd. "Remember how George said he wasn't in charge? How's Peashooter any different?"

"That's enough!"

*"Any fool can make a rule, and any fool will mind it!"*

"You think you can use Thoreau against me?"

To the camp, I said, "Peashooter promises you the world, but then suddenly there's a pop quiz!"

"This is for the birds." Capone got up from his log and marched toward the fire pit. "I'm sick of listening to all this crap. This place is worse than it was before."

Getting straight into Peashooter's face, Capone asked, "What if we don't want to go to your stupid class anymore?"

Peashooter stared back with his cold gray eyes. "Nobody's forcing you,"

Capone grinned. His braces glowed orange in the weak firelight, like molten train tracks. He leaned even farther into Peashooter's face.

He completely failed to notice Compass standing behind him.

"Capone!" I yelled.

Too late. Compass kicked Capone in the soft joint of his left leg. He landed on his knees in front of Peashooter. "Hold him down."

Sporkboy and Compass each grabbed an arm and held Capone in place.

"Let go of me." Capone struggled to free himself.

"You've got two choices," Peashooter said. "Option A— kneel. Or Option B . . ."

". . . I punch you in the face?"

Peashooter pulled out a pair of pliers from his back pocket.

"Hold *really* still."

Peashooter opened and closed the rusty metal pincers. The campers all watched as he pinched Capone's cheeks with his free hand and squeezed.

"Stop," Capone managed to mutter through his smushed mouth.

"*Ssssssh* . . ." Peashooter sealed his pliers around the top steel bracket fastened to Capone's central incisor. "I need to concentrate."

Capone's eyes widened. His sweat glistened in the light of the fire.

"This may hurt a bit. . . ."

The trees shuddered with Capone's screams.

Peashooter raised the pliers above his head. They held onto a single bracket, a knot of crooked wire snaking out.

"One down." Peashooter exhaled. "Nineteen more to go. . . ."

Capone squealed. The shrill pitch caused Peashooter to pull back and pause.

"Is there something you would like to say?" Peashooter asked, still holding Capone by his mouth.

Capone quickly nodded, red drool dribbling down his chin. "You're the king," he managed to sputter between his staccato inhales.

"What's that?" Peashooter cupped his hand to his ear and leaned in closer.

*"You're the king, you're the king, you're the king!"*

Peashooter motioned for Sporkboy and Compass to let Capone go. He landed next to my cage, reduced to a blubbering bundle.

"Put him with the counselors." Peashooter wiped off his pliers before regarding the rest of the amphitheater. "So . . . where were we?"

Nobody said a word.

"Ah, yes. Time to do away with those who seek to undermine our Tribe."

# PENDLETON VS. THE TRIBE

**P**eashooter was now perched atop a lifeguard chair that had been dragged in from the shores of Lake Wendigo.

Perfect, I thought. Peashooter has his own throne now.

In his hand, he tightly gripped a handmade gavel—the empty shell of a snapping turtle tied around the end of a gardening trowel.

Yardstick and Compass stood at either side of his chair. Each brandished a gardening tool pilfered from the camp's equipment shed. Compass had a telescoping tree-branch pruner. Yardstick carried some kind of aerator with four separately spinning blades for piercing the soil.

*Or human flesh.*

I tried making eye contact with Yardstick as Sporkboy prodded me before the fire pit, but he wouldn't look at me.

I didn't like the looks of this.

The bonfire was blazing once more, compliments of Firefly. There wouldn't be anything left of the camp for Firefly to burn at the rate he was going.

My sunburned compatriots flinched as Peashooter hammered the snapping turtle's shell against the armrest of his chair—*bang, bang, bang.* To be honest, everybody had been acting pretty jumpy ever since Capone disappeared.

"We have called you all here," Peashooter announced, "to put Mr. Spencer Pendleton on trial."

This was news to me. "On what charges?"

"*Treason.* You have betrayed your Tribe. We follow the Law of Claw and Fang and you have broken it with your disloyalty!"

"*The law will never make men free,*" I said, quoting Thoreau. "*It is men who have got to make the law free.*"

"Silence!" Peashooter shouted. I could tell I was under his skin like a tick. "You will be judged by a jury of your fellow peers."

"How's that supposed to be fair? Everybody here wants to kill me!"

"If you prefer," Compass suggested, "you could forgo a trial by jury and have the honorable judge Peashooter decide your fate. Bet that'd be one speedy trial."

I agreed. "I'll take the jury, thanks."

"After much deliberation," Peashooter announced, "it has been decided that select members of cabins three and four shall stand in for our jury."

I spun around and found my bunkmates all huddled together on their log. None of them would meet my eyes.

"What kind of jury selection was that?" I cried. "You have to interview your jurors to make sure that they can be impartial. You can't just pick and choose!"

"Bring it up with your defense attorney."

"Who's representing me?"

"Any volunteers? Will one of you defend Pendleton?"

Nobody.

"Guess I'm representing myself."

"Let the record show that Mr. Pendleton refused counsel and—"

"I didn't refuse." I cut Peashooter off. "Nobody wanted to—"

"He refused counsel and elected *to represent himself.*"

"So who am I going up against?"

Compass stepped forward, the crust of calamine lotion flaking off from his face like a snake shedding its skin. "You're looking at the prosecution right here."

"*You?*" I couldn't help but guffaw.

A broiling red cloud of acne darkened his face, burning through the lingering pink calamine cumulus. "I've got two years on the debate team under my belt, which is more than you can say."

I lifted my chin up. "Well, I've got to warn you—*debate*'s my middle name."

"Yeah—and *dead*'s your first and *meat*'s your last."

"My name's Dead Debate Meat? Leave the comebacks to me, Compass."

"Say that again, I dare you—"

It looked like Compass wanted to sock me right in the eye. That would've meant a mistrial and this kangaroo court would've come to an abrupt halt.

Peashooter hammered his gavel, snapping Compass out of it. "Shall we begin?"

I nodded to Compass. "Let's do this."

After countless hours of watching courtroom dramas on the boob tube, you'd assume I would have absorbed some sort of law degree—but nope. Not even close.

Sporkboy stood before Peashooter, cleared his throat, and called—"All rise."

The cannibals stood.

"Court is now in session," Sporkboy cried. "The honorable Judge Peashooter presiding."

"Please be seated," Peashooter said. I sat down. "Will the defendant rise."

Suddenly everyone's eyes were on me.

"That's you," Sporkboy whispered.

"Right." I stood back up, unsure of myself. "Of course."

Sporkboy gave me a warm smile. "Thanks again for saving my—"

"Bailiff," Peashooter cut him off.

The smile across Sporkboy's lips withered. He cleared his

throat and said—"Raise your right hand, please, and place your left on the book."

Looking down, I discovered Sporkboy was holding a tattered copy of *The Call of the Wild.* I pressed my palm against the book's cover.

Sporkboy raced through the words so fast I could hardly make out what he said. "Doyousolemnlysweartotellthetruththe wholetruthsohelpyouGod?"

"As long as I get a fair trial."

Sporkboy looked to Peashooter to see if this was admissible. He nodded.

"Does the defendant understand the charge of treason that has been brought against him?" Peashooter asked. "If so, how do you plead?"

"Uh—how about *so very not guilty?*"

"Prosecutor, the floor is yours to make your opening arguments."

Compass circled the fire pit in his most rehearsed lawyer-walk. "Members of the jury. The Rat you see before you may look like just another runt of the litter, but believe me—Spencer Pendleton is not your friend, he is not your ally. He is not one of us at all."

Compass halted right where he stood. He flung his arm out at his side, brandishing his index finger straight at me as if to aim a gun at my head.

"He is . . . *a war criminal!*"

"Hold on a sec," I said, rising. "Isn't that taking this a little too far . . . ?"

"We are at war, Mr. Pendleton—are we not? War with the status quo!"

"Yeah, up until your Tribe *became* the status quo."

"It's my turn for opening arguments—"

"The Tribe is . . . *dedicated to maintenance of the status quo*," I quoted Martin Luther King Jr.

"Objection!"

"Your leader," I said, "*the honorable Peashooter*, warps the words of others to get you to do his bidding. The *real* words, the *actual* written words, aren't enough—so he bends them to say whatever the heck he wants them to say."

"Objection!"

"I may make a lot of enemies, but at least I'm telling the truth."

"Your honor," Compass pleaded with Peashooter, "I strongly object to this! How can I make my arguments if the defendant continues to speak at will?"

"Sustained," Peashooter said. "Hold your tongue until it's your turn, Mr. Pendleton—or I'll have Sporkboy staple your lips shut."

I knew lawyers could get thrown into jail for being in contempt of court, but lip-stapling was new for me. I figured it was best to keep my mouth shut.

"Proceed, prosecutor," Peashooter instructed.

Compass turned back to me, a snide grin spreading over

his face. "Peashooter is not the one on trial here today, Mr. Pendleton. *You are.* And the crimes you have committed are very clear. You ratted us out . . . *to a parent!*"

"That's not true! I mean—*objection!*"

"Overruled," Peashooter droned.

"Not just any parent," Compass kept going, "but one of the Tribe's own. You deliberately went behind the Tribe's back and visited Sully Tulliver's father."

Hearing Sully's name out loud made my chest tighten.

"Well, yeah." I stumbled over my own words. "But I didn't tell—"

"Do you deny informing Mr. Tulliver of the whereabouts of his daughter?"

"Yeah, but—"

"Do you deny informing him that his daughter was in fact still alive when he had believed she had been dead?"

"He had the right to know—"

"Let the record show that Mr. Pendleton has confessed to favoring an *outsider* over his own Tribe. *A parent!* Even though he was fully aware of tribal laws regarding the fraternizing with interlopers, he chose to acknowledge the existence of our private society—breaking not one, but *two* laws at the same time. Associating with an adult is to associate with the enemy, Mr. Pendleton—and that is treason!"

*Quick. Think fast, Spencer. Hit him back before you lose your ground.*

"Fine," I said. "Then I'd like to call a witness to testify on my behalf."

"Call as many witnesses as you like," Peashooter shrugged.

"I call . . . *you*, Peashooter!" I flung my index finger at him. Charles gasped.

"Order in the court!" Peashooter shouted, hammering his homemade gavel against his armrest. "Mr. Pendleton, it's highly impracticable for a judge to be called as a witness for a trial he himself is presiding over."

"What are you afraid of? I thought your conscience was clean. Or is there something you don't want to say under oath in a court of tribal law?"

"All right—I'll allow it. But you're on a short leash, Mr. Pendleton. *Very short.*"

I waited until I knew I had everyone's attention. I cleared my throat. "Do you think your mother misses you?"

Peashooter was taken back by the question. "I don't see what that has to do with these proceedings, Mr. Pendleton."

"Let me rephrase the question: What if your mom was looking for you right now? What if she was searching for answers to what had happened to her son?"

"Don't bring my mother into this."

"What do you think would break her heart more? Never knowing what had happened to her son—or finding you out here, in the woods, alive and well?"

Peashooter remained silent for a little too long.

Campers started looking toward one another.

"Well, Peashooter?"

I could see an idea blossom in his brain. "I believe Peter Pan said it best." He recited—"*Long ago . . . I thought like you that my mother would always keep the window open for me, so I stayed away for moons and moons and moons, and then flew back; but the window was barred, for mother had forgotten all about me. . . .*"

"Bet your mom misses you right now."

"That's enough."

"I'm sure all of your parents are wondering how you are. . . ."

"Order in the court!"

"What if he's right?" Sporkboy asked.

"*Order!*" The bone-hard *thwonk* of the empty turtle shell echoed until everyone was quiet. "*Order!*"

Compass stood from his log. "If it pleases the court, your honor, I make the motion that we move to a verdict now."

"Objection!" I shouted. "I strongly object!"

"Overruled." Peashooter composed himself before nodding at Klepto. "Mr. Foreman, has the jury reached a verdict?"

"How could they?" I asked, completely incredulous.

Klepto stood up and cleared his throat. "Sir . . ."

"Is it a unanimous vote?" Peashooter asked.

Klepto's lazy eye wandered off on its own, afraid to make eye contact with Peashooter. "It is not, your honor."

Peashooter didn't seemed pleased by this. "Mr. Foreman, we need a unanimous vote in order to reach a verdict."

"We know, your honor. We did exactly like you said, but . . ."

"But—*what*?"

"There's still one jury member who voted against the rest of us."

"Who?"

All the jury members turned toward . . .

. . . *Charles.*

He kept his eyes on his feet, chin dipped to his chest.

Peashooter zeroed in on him. "Stand up."

Charles slowly rose, his eyes never leaving the ground.

"Your name—your tribal name, the name we gave you—is Jaws, isn't it?"

Charles barely nodded.

"Have you made up your mind?"

He nodded again.

"And what's your verdict?"

". . . Innocent?" The word was so small, so fragile—it sounded like a newly born hatchling, blind and featherless.

"*Innocent?*" Peashooter asked. "Even when everyone else says he's guilty?"

Charles nodded again.

"And what makes you believe Mr. Pendleton is so *innocent*?"

Charles muttered something I couldn't make out. Apparently, neither could Peashooter. "I'm sorry . . . Say that again?"

"He's my friend."

"Friend?" Peashooter huffed. "He used to be my friend, too. I trusted him. But do you know what he did? He betrayed us by favoring somebody's *father* over his own Tribe. Do you think your *friend* wouldn't do the same to you?"

Charles didn't respond.

"Tell me, Jaws . . . what exactly has Mr. Pendleton done that makes you believe he's your *friend*?"

"He . . . he shares a bunk with me. I mean, we used to share a bunk."

"And?"

"And . . . he talks to me. Sometimes."

"Sometimes," Peashooter said, "in order to serve the greater good of the Tribe, certain exceptions must be made in regards to our own laws. That's why, if the jury cannot reach a unanimous decision, we'll have a hung jury on our hands."

Then, directly to Charles, he asked: "Do you know what a hung jury is?"

Charles shook his head no.

"A hung jury means anyone who doesn't vote with the majority will be taken to the flagpole up front and hung for as long as it takes him to change his mind."

*I'm no law expert, but I'm pretty sure that's not what a "hung jury" means.*

Charles finally looked up from the ground, shocked at the threat. His badger mandibles swung open as if to say something.

But the words just weren't there.

"So what say you?" Peashooter prodded. "Have you made up your mind?"

Charles dropped his eyes once more and bit his lower lip. Blood rose up. "Guilty, your honor."

"Louder," Peashooter insisted.

"Guilty."

"Louder."

"*Guilty!*"

The word echoed through the woods, and Charles slumped back onto his log, defeated. I watched his shoulders shudder, as if he were dry-heaving.

Peashooter grinned. "Mr. Foreman—have you reached a verdict *now?*"

"We most certainly have, your honor," Klepto said, beaming. "On the charge of treason, we find the defendant . . . *guilty!*"

"Let it be noted that on this day," Peashooter called out, "this court has found Mr. Spencer Pendleton, our one and only Rat, *guilty* of treason against his Tribe."

All the campers in the amphitheater cheered.

I bolted from my seat. "But—but that's not fair!"

"Your honor, due to the sensitive nature of this case," Compass interjected, "I recommend we proceed to sentencing right away."

Peashooter nodded. "Motion to proceed to sentencing has been granted."

"You can't do this!"

Sporkboy prodded me forward with his quarterstaff. I fell to my knees before Peashooter's high chair.

Peashooter hammered his snapping turtle gavel against the armrest so hard, I heard its shell crack.

"Spencer Pendleton," he called out. "For crimes of treason against your Tribe, you are hereby sentenced to death by . . . *tribal triathlon.*"

# FAHRENHEIT 451

ood evening, cannibals," Peashooter's voice cut through the night air. *"The blood-longing became stronger than ever before. He was a killer . . ."*

If only there was a way to tune out his voice, I thought.

*Earplugs. My kingdom for a pair of earplugs. . . .*

I turned toward the dying embers of the bonfire, fueled by the last bits of kindling from the bunk bed I had slept in for only one night.

*". . . surviving triumphantly in a hostile environment where only the strong survived,"* Peashooter continued to recite through the PA system. I could hear him flip the page, the sound of paper gently grazing over paper—then nothing.

Why had he stopped? Peashooter must've fallen asleep.

Silence. The amphitheater felt empty.

Almost empty.

I heard a rustling above my cage. Looking up, I discovered the Piranhas scattered amongst the branches. They had climbed into the trees, silently observing.

"Any chance you guys would want to help a fellow break out, would you?"

Firefly rushed into the amphitheater, a pair of bamboo tiki torches slung across his back. Ashen fingerprints speckled his face, and his hands were covered in soot.

Something was stuffed under his arm.

Both arms.

I could hear him muttering. "Gotta feed the flames, gotta feed the flames."

What was he carrying?

*Books.*

He had a stack of books crammed under each arm.

*My books.*

"Mason," I shouted. "You can't burn those!"

"Gotta feed the flames," he strained, unable to control himself. "Gotta feed the flames, gotta feed the flames . . ."

"Peashooter said no books!"

But he wasn't listening.

The boy named Mason had long since been incinerated, his mind irrevocably reduced to cinders.

And like a phoenix rising out from the ashes, Firefly was all that was left.

"Feed the flames, feed the flames, feed the flames . . ."

He dropped all of the books onto the ground before the fire. He unsheathed the tiki torches from over his shoulders, like a pair of samurai swords, swinging them through the air before driving their wicked tips into the fire. Once they were lit, he staked the bamboo into the soil—then picked a book from the pile.

*Lord of the Flies.*

Firefly flipped to a random page and read—"*'Cos the smoke's a signal and we can't be rescued if we don't have smoke.*"

He tore out the page, balled it up before my face—and tossed it into the fire.

"Stop!"

Firefly ripped out another page. And another. He held each one up in front of my cage before crumpling it in his hand and feeding it to the flames.

Before long, the book jacket was empty. All that was left was a tattered spine, a few loose shreds of paper clinging to the book's backbone.

Then Firefly tossed that into the fire, too.

*Watership Down* was next.

The bonfire lapped up each page until there was nothing.

All I could do was watch each page vanish. Each tear felt like a paper cut across my chest. I couldn't take this torture much longer. But there was the rest of my library left to go, and I had no doubt Firefly intended on burning every last one.

Firefly held up *The Outsiders*. He tore out a page and expertly folded it into a paper airplane. He dipped the tip of his S. E. Hinton 747 into the tiki torch's flame. He launched his burning airplane through the air, aiming its nose directly at my cage.

It crash-landed at my feet. I had to stomp it out before my cage caught on fire.

Firefly had already folded his next airplane by the time I had put out the first. He lit its nose on fire with the tiki torch, launched it—and ripped out another page.

"Firefly—stop it!"

A fleet of flaming kamikaze paper airplanes kept crashing into my cage, and all I could do was bat them down before they could ignite my flammable cell.

"Gotta feed the flames," Firefly mumbled as he ripped a fresh page free.

It started to rain.

Just a light sprinkle, extinguishing the tiki torches.

Then I noticed how I wasn't getting wet. The drizzle seemed to be aimed specifically at Firefly. The downpour redirected itself from his hand up to his head.

We both looked up, probably coming to the same conclusion simultaneously with one another—*that's not rain.*

The Piranhas peered down from the trees, proudly presenting their natural fire extinguishers.

Firefly leapt out of the way—but it was too late. He was completely doused. He just froze, unable to move. He simply held his arms out at his sides and dripped.

Compass entered the amphitheater with his quarterstaff.

"What's going on in here?" Spotting the Piranhas, he jabbed at the tree and sent them scurrying away. "Get out of here! Get!"

One whiff of Firefly, and Compass flinched.

"What happened to you?"

Firefly only bowed his head. "Gotta keep the bonfire going."

"Go take a shower," Compass instructed. "Wash yourself off before anyone else smells you."

Firefly raced out from the amphitheater, nearly in tears, leaving me alone with Compass.

"Everybody's starting to unravel," I said. "You know that, right?"

"Prisoners only speak when spoken to."

I let out a half-laugh. "You guys have turned into camp counselors of chaos."

"Take that back."

Yardstick rushed into the amphitheater, out of breath. "Somebody set the totem pole on fire!"

*If Firefly can't bring the kindling to the fire, he'll bring the fire to the kindling.*

"Does Peashooter know?" Compass asked.

"He's asleep," Yardstick said. "I figured I'd tell you first before waking him."

"I'll find Sporkboy. We can put it out before Firefly sets the rest of the camp on fire."

Yardstick and I both watched Compass exit the amphitheater.

As soon as he was gone, Yardstick turned to me. "Ready to get the heck out of here?"

"You don't have to ask me twice," I said.

Something shiny dropped at Yardstick's feet. My eyes locked onto it.

An X-ACTO blade.

I picked it up and started slicing. The shoestrings had been tightly wound around the joints, the branches knotted at each corner.

Yardstick kept a lookout. "Hurry."

"I'm trying," I muttered. The shoestring finally unraveled from the branch. I grabbed hold and yanked as hard as I could, prying the piece of wood free.

I slipped my head through the gap, only for my shoulders to jam.

*Too tight.*

I had to pull myself back in and keep cutting. Working on the neighboring bar, I muttered under my breath—"Come on, come on, come on."

The shoestring started to give.

"Someone's coming," Yardstick said.

The lace loosened, then snapped free.

"It's Compass!"

There was no time to cut through the other end of the bar. I wedged myself into the gap. My shoulders slipped through. I was just about to clear the cage when my shirt snagged on the end of a branch. I had to reach back and yank myself free.

Compass walked into the amphitheater just as I plunged from the cage.

"Well, this is awkward," I said.

"How did you—?"

Yardstick thumped Compass upside the head with his quarterstaff. Compass went cross-eyed before falling to the ground.

Yardstick winced. "Sorry . . ."

I noticed the Piranhas had returned to their perch in the tree and pressed my finger against my lips. They nodded.

"Grab his legs," I said to Yardstick as I leapt to my feet. "Compass needs a time out."

$$\bullet \bullet \bullet$$

Firefly had offered up the perfect distraction. While everyone else focused on extinguishing the flaming totem pole, Yardstick and I could slip out from the amphitheater totally unnoticed. A processional of cannibals rushed up the path, each carrying a bucket full of water from Lake Wendigo, while we kept to the tree line.

I halted long enough to watch the totem pole get doused. Those six blackened skulls were charred beyond recognition, the outer layer of bark burned away.

"We've got to go," Yardstick whispered. "*Now.*"

"Keep an eye out for me, okay?"

"Where are you going? The woods are this way."

"All I need is one second," I said, and ran for cabin two.

No guards. The door was surprisingly unlocked.

This was way too easy, I thought as I entered.

All the lightbulbs had been removed inside. Darkness enveloped every corner. A sliver of moonlight reached in through the window, barely illuminating the pack of discombobulated counselors stretched out along the furniture-free floor. They looked like a litter of newborn puppies, still blind to the world. Defenseless.

"George?" I whispered. "Stan? Anybody?"

"Spencer . . . ?" A hoarse voice struggled out from the dark. "Is that you?"

"Who's that?"

"Stan . . ." He didn't sound like The Man anymore.

"Can you guys get up? Can you run?"

Their heads lolled over their shoulders, back and forth. I spotted Capone curled up on the floor amongst the rest.

"Come on!" I grabbed his leg and tugged. "Get up! On your feet! Let's go!"

He wouldn't budge. None of them would.

"Now's not the time to lay around." I tugged Capone toward the door. "We've got to—"

I turned to find Peashooter standing in the doorway.

The entire Tribe waited behind him.

Yardstick was on his knees, arms bound behind his back with

bungee cords. Compass and Sporkboy stood at his sides, making sure he didn't move.

"Gotta hand it to you, Rat," Peashooter said. "I didn't think you had it in you."

*"How can any man be weak who dares to be at all?"*

"Glad to hear you've been reading."

"I've had a lot of time to kill."

*"As if you could kill time without injuring eternity,"* Peashooter recited.

I pounced on Peashooter and pressed the X-ACTO blade against his throat. So much for nonviolence, but my back was up against the wall here.

Peashooter held out his hands at his sides, remaining calm.

"Let's take this very slow," I said. "Or you'll never quote Thoreau again."

"I've read it so many times, I don't quote it . . . *I am it*."

"You really should get out more."

"Where would I go?" he asked. "This is my home now."

This was what happens when you lose yourself in a book . . . *completely*. Now he'll never come back.

"What should we do?" Compass asked.

Even with a blade pressed to his neck, Peashooter couldn't help but grin. "You heard him. . . . What should we do now, Rat?"

I spotted Charles in the crowd, a strained expression spread across his face. Klepto stood next to him, his bow and arrow slung over his shoulder. He took it into his hands, itching for a shot.

"Don't test me," I said.

"This is all a test," Peashooter said. "Every day is a test."

"Keep your initiations for someone else. Release the counselors."

"Or what?" Peashooter was unnervingly calm. "They've always been free to go. The door has always been unlocked. They've just never been motivated to leave."

It dawned on me that Klepto would have generously donated his tackle box of pilfered prescriptions. I was betting all of the adults had been dunked under dosage after dosage of mood stabilizers.

Peashooter nodded at Klepto. "Can you take him down?"

Klepto pinched his lazy eye shut, taking aim. "Easily."

"Do it."

Before Klepto could fire, Charles sunk his teeth into his wrist. Klepto howled as his fingers released the bowstring. The arrow struck the cabin door just behind my shoulder.

Klepto jerked his arm back, but Charles refused to let him go, the two playing tug-of-war with Klepto's own wrist.

Once Charles's badger mandibles locked in place, there's no releasing them.

"Get him!" Peashooter shouted. "Get him now!"

I shoved him out of the door and rushed back inside the cabin.

Charles finally let Klepto go. "Run, Spencer," he yelled before being buried beneath a pile of his chemically imbalanced compatriots.

I slammed the cabin door and pressed my back against it.

"All right, guys," I shouted. "Time to wake up!"

Fists began to pound against the door at my back.

"I could really use a little help here. . . ."

The door budged behind me. My feet skidded forward a few inches.

"Now or never, guys . . . Motivate! Motivate!"

The door gave way behind me and I was pushed to the floor.

Rolling onto my back, I saw that Peashooter had forced his way in. A pair of cannibals thrust Charles and Yardstick into the cabin. They landed on top of me.

"So much for your big prison break." Peashooter leaned against the door frame. "Better get some rest, boys. You'll need it for tomorrow."

The door slammed, sealing us inside the pitch-black. This time Peashooter locked the door—*CLICK!*

"Sorry, Spencer." Charles bowed his head. "I tried. . . ."

"If it wasn't for you," I said, "I'd have an arrow buried between my eyes."

"That's it, then," Yardstick said. "We're dead."

"Not yet," I mustered. But the words held no weight.

"Spencer?" A weak voice whispered my name. My eyes adjusted to discover George on the floor. No more ponytail. "Who are those kids out there?"

"My imaginary friends."

# TRIBAL TRIATHLON

**P**eashooter loomed large over the rest of the Tribe. The PA system's mic had been rigged with extra cable, allowing him to stand on the cabin's roof.

Charles, Yardstick, and I were dragged out from the brig and brought to our knees before him, our hands bungee-corded behind our backs.

Peashooter lifted his arms into the air, summoning the camp to chant—"Claw and Fang!"

"Claw and Fang!"

"Claw and Fang!"

Peashooter dropped his arms, and the cheering instantly died out. He brought the microphone up and began to preach. "Some amongst us would prefer we remained enslaved. Imprisoned by our parents. Kept in line with our prescriptions."

Peashooter pointed directly at me.

"For one of our own to oppose our charge and side with the adults of this world, well—there is no word for that person other than rat. Say it—*Rat!*"

"Rat!" the crowd roared.

"Rat!"

"Rat!"

"And there is only one appropriate punishment for rats—*Death!*"

"Death!"

"Death!"

"Death!"

"Today, we sentence three such conspirators. You have all been found guilty for committing crimes against your Tribe. Any last requests?"

"I am *the Wild*," I stared straight at Peashooter and recited. "*. . . the unknown, the terrible, the ever menacing, the thing that prowled in the darkness around the fires of the primeval world . . .*"

"Enough," Peashooter turned to his fans. "Everyone ready for an execution?"

The crowd cheered.

"What's the fun in merely executing your enemies? Today, you will all hunt. Take a good look at your prey."

I glanced over at Charles. Tears streaked his cheeks. Yardstick kept his chin tucked into his chest. His eyes never left the ground.

"You will be given a fifteen-minute head start," Peashooter

announced. "If you make it out of these woods alive, then congrats. You're free to go. Best of luck."

I really didn't like the sound of that.

"What happens when somebody believes they are about to die? They cry out for their mommy and daddy. Well, mommy and daddy aren't coming to save you today. No one is. Cannibals—it's time!"

I saw Compass slip a pillowcase over Charles's head. I caught one final millisecond of panic in his eyes before I was enveloped in a white blindness.

"Must be lonely in there." Compass's voice seeped through the cotton shroud. "How about some company?"

He slipped something inside the pillowcase. I peered down my nose and discovered he was holding a glass jar just beneath my chin.

Something buzzed against the glass.

*Wings?*

A wasp rose up from the opening, hovering in front of my face. Compass quickly pulled the jar out and sealed the pillowcase around my neck.

*The wasp. Was inside. My pillowcase.*

It grazed along the cotton contours, looking for a hole to fly out of, finding absolutely nothing but my face.

He didn't seem all too happy to be trapped in here with me.

*The feeling's mutual.*

Somebody gave me a swift kick in the rear end.

"And they're off!" Peashooter's voice echoed over the intercom.

I was running blindly through the woods. My feet couldn't move fast enough. I shook my head in every which direction in hopes of throwing off the pillowcase.

The wasp's wings brushed against my right cheek.

*Please don't sting me Mr. Wasp, please don't sting. . . .*

I couldn't free my hands. The bungee cord wouldn't budge. I kept wriggling my wrists, growing numb from the loss of circulation.

*If I could just slip my thumb through, I think I might be able to—*

There was a blur of yellow directly before my eyes. That wasp plopped itself on my forehead. I didn't stop running. I could feel my pace pick up, racing faster.

Faster.

*If I could just free one finger, just one—*

I ran face-first into something sturdy.

A tree.

I fell over backward, hitting the ground. I had to blink a couple dozen times to bring my equilibrium back.

I yanked my left hand free from my bungee-bonds and pulled off my pillowcase. The wasp was now a yellow jam spread across my forehead.

I winced from the brightness of the sun.

Looking up, I saw the trees were shimmering in the sunlight.

Something metallic.

Cell phones. The busted guts of a dozen cell phones dangled from the branches. I jumped up and plucked one.

*Please work, please just work, please—*

No good. The screen was cracked, the batteries plucked out from the back. A nail had been driven directly through the keypad and tied off with a piece of twine.

I had to run. I took a step forward and quickly came face-to-face with . . .

*. . . Myself?*

A black-and-white photocopy of my yearbook picture had been tacked to a tree trunk. I could tell from the pained expression on my face—part discomfiture, part constipation, caught in mid-blink. Mom had a million of these back at home.

Each eye was crossed out with a red *X*. At the bottom, someone had written:

## MISSING.

I spotted another flyer. Same *X*'ed out eyeballs:

## HAVE YOU SEEN THIS BOY?

I was surrounded by dozens of my own duplicated dead-eyed face, each one awkwardly smiling back at me. There was another:

## LAST SEEN THIS SUMMER.

Charles and Yardstick were still blindly struggling through the woods, their heads swallowed by their pillowcases. It was like watching a game of pinball. They would rebound off the trees, stumble back onto their feet, and run all over again, only to hit another tree.

"Yardstick—stop!" I called after him. "It's me!"

He wouldn't listen, plowing ahead. I had to chase after him.

"Stop running!"

I jumped into the air and yanked off his pillowcase. He looked stunned. And stung. Several welts pockmarked his forehead. His chest heaved from all the panic.

"You okay?"

"Not really." He scanned the woods, hyperventilating. "We don't have much time until they're right on top of us."

"What do we do?"

"*Haul ass.*"

Charles had just puckered up to another trunk, running head-on in to a tree. He rebounded off the bark and staggered back. Shaking his pillowcased head, Charles collided with the same tree all over again.

And again.

"Let's get him before the others do," I said.

"Careful." Yardstick grabbed my arm. "These woods are booby-trapped."

"*Booby-trapped?* With what?"

"You don't want to know."

Charles had managed to make his way back onto his feet. He took one blind step in a different direction and . . .

*SNAP!*

A set of steel, *ahem*, jaws latched themselves around Charles's shin. He let out an ear-piercing shriek as he fell over face-first onto the ground.

Yardstick and I rushed up.

A leg-hold trap had closed around Charles's left ankle. The metal teeth had sunk deep in his Achilles tendon.

I pulled the pillowcase off his head. Charles's face was a portrait of pain. When he looked down at his foot, his eyes widened even further. He shrieked.

I picked up a nearby stick and pushed it past Charles's lips. "Bite."

Charles sunk his teeth in. The stick instantly snapped in half. I found another, thicker stick—"Try not to bite down so hard this time, okay?"

Charles limply nodded.

"How many traps are out here?"

"This is nothing," Yardstick said. "There're land mines, trip wires, snares, pitfalls . . ."

I motioned to Charles's bloodied leg. "What should we do?"

"Let him chew through his own leg and free himself?"

Charles squealed, vigorously shaking his head.

"You grab that end," I nodded to the trap. "I'll grab the other. On the count of three, pull as hard as you can. Charles—when you're free, pull your leg out of the way. Once we let go, those teeth are gonna snap shut—*hard*. Got it?"

Charles nodded, clenching his teeth around the stick.

"Okay, here we go," I said.

We all took a deep breath.

"One," Yardstick and I started the countdown together. "Two . . ."

"Wait, wait, wait," I interrupted.

Charles moaned.

"Is it one, two, and *then* pull on three? Or is it one, two, three, *and then* pull?"

Yardstick thought it through. "One, two, three *and* pull."

"Just wanted to be sure."

Charles bore his pitiful eyes right through me.

"Okay," Yardstick started again. "One . . . two . . . three. *Pull!*"

It took all our strength just to wrench its metallic mouth open. The spring coiled within the trap squeaked as we pried its jaws back.

"Now!" I demanded. "Lift your leg out now before—"

Charles managed to yank his foot out of the way before my fingers slipped. The trap snapped back shut with a loud metallic—*CLANG!*

Charles gripped his shin and rolled over the ground. He was bleeding pretty badly. I pulled off my shirt and created the best tourniquet I could, cinching it off.

"We've got to get him help," I said.

"We've got to help ourselves!" Yardstick half-shouted. "There's an entire tribe of chemically imbalanced kids coming this way."

"So what do we do?"

Yardstick looked to Charles. "Leave him. That'll buy us some time."

"Don't leave me," Charles whined. "Please, *please* don't leave me!"

I looked at Yardstick. "You can't be serious."

"He's dead weight," Yardstick said. "That means we'd be dead, too!"

"We can't leave him here."

Yardstick looked at me as if I had lost my mind.

A low rumble echoed from farther off in the woods. The sound of sputtering turbines hacking to life clamored through the trees.

"Is that a lawnmower?" I asked.

Panic blanched Yardstick's face. "Move. *Now.*" Yardstick grabbed Charles by his left arm while I took the right, carrying him through the woods.

Charles felt like a sack of potatoes. "I knew you wouldn't leave me. . . ."

"Don't thank me yet." I noticed Charles was still bleeding. Red dollops dappled our path like a trail of crimson bread crumbs.

The snarl of a small engine grew louder.

What is that? I asked myself.

Yardstick glanced over his shoulder. "They're gaining on us," he yelled. "Watch out for pitfalls."

"Watch out for pit—?"

The ground gave way underneath my feet.

I was plummeting into the hollow earth.

*Found that pitfall.*

Yardstick immediately dug his heels into the ground and clamped both hands around Charles's arm. When the slack in Charles's shoulders tightened, my body stopped its free fall. I was suddenly hovering in the air, still clasping Charles's hand.

That hungry hole was about ten feet deep. Its open mouth had been covered with a latticework of branches and leaves to conceal its perilous plunge. The pit's floor was lined with flesh-piercing spikes fashioned from broomsticks.

Looking up, I saw Yardstick on his stomach, holding on to Charles. Charles had no choice but to serve as my lifeline.

"*Owwwww!*" Charles's shoulder popped. "I think I just dislocated my arm."

I clawed my way up. "Just don't let go. . . ."

"You're the one holding on to me!"

"Climb up quick," Yardstick strained. The veins in his neck looked as if they were about to snap. "I'm losing . . . my grip."

I had to plant my heel into the nape of Charles's neck to gain the leverage to climb the rest of the way out. "Sorry," I said as I scrambled onto solid ground.

Yardstick pulled Charles back onto his feet. We both noticed Charles's arm dangled at an awkward angle, loosely flapping about.

"That doesn't look right," I said.

Before Charles could resist, Yardstick took the limp limb into his hands.

*POP!*

Yardstick pushed Charles's arm upward, returning his humerus to its proper socket. Charles shrieked again and collapsed.

Yardstick followed alongside him.

Then me.

The three of us lay quiet for a moment, not saying a word. I could hear that familiar wheeze in my throat.

*Now is really not the time for an asthma attack. . . .*

"Here," Yardstick reached into his back pocket. "I've got something for you."

My Little Friend.

I grabbed it and immediately freshened my airways. "Anyone else wanna puff?" I asked.

I passed my inhaler to Yardstick, who took a quick spritz. "Thanks."

Charles, too. He retched. "This stuff tastes like a rusted penny roll."

"Remind me again. What are we supposed to be keeping our eyes out for?"

"Land mines," Yardstick listed off. "Trip wires, snares, pitfalls, mantraps . . ."

*"Weed whackers!"* Klepto vaulted out from behind a tree, brandishing his own string trimmer as if the machine had never been intended to snip wildflowers.

But fingers. Or ears. Or noses.

Anything he felt like pruning.

"Thomas—please," I tried reasoning with him. "This has got to stop."

"The name's Klepto." He gave the pull cord on his whipper-snipper a good yank. Its engine coughed out a puff of exhaust, but didn't catch. "Now's the part where you guys run and I chase you."

"GO!" Yardstick leapt back up onto his feet and pulled Charles up with him. I grabbed Charles's free arm and hoofed it.

I could hear Klepto tug on the cord just over my shoulder—only this time, the engine caught, hacking and spitting to life.

Yardstick and I did our best three-legged race with five feet.

"Faster!" Yardstick shouted.

Klepto howled like a wolf behind us. There was no reasoning with him now. All we could do was run.

*Faster. Faster. Faster.*

"Keep close to the trees," Yardstick barked.

We couldn't outrace him. Not on foot. Not with Charles.

"This way," Yardstick shouted.

"Which way?"

"Left!"

Too late. I stepped to the right. Charles's arms stretched as I went one way and Yardstick went the other.

I felt a trip wire catch my shin, triggering a large rock tied to an overhanging branch.

There wasn't enough time to react. All I could do was watch

this pendulum descend from the tree in a crushing arc.

I was whipped to my right, limp as a rag doll. Yardstick had yanked Charles, who had, in turn, pulled me out of the way.

Another second and that chunk of granite would have collided with my nose.

Klepto wasn't as lucky.

He had been on our heels. Too close to duck. The rock swung directly into his face, bowling him over onto the ground. The weed whacker sputtered out from his hands.

"Maybe we should help—" I started, but Yardstick pressed his palm over my mouth and pushed me against a tree.

He held a finger up to his lips. The sound of feet stampeding through the undergrowth grew louder.

Several bodies blurred between the trees. Each brandished a spear.

"Where'd they go?" somebody whispered.

"They were here just a second ago. . . ."

"This way."

Yardstick kept his palm over my mouth until we could hear the pack wander farther off.

"Wha . . . ?" Klepto moaned at our feet. "Mffm . . ."

Yardstick motioned in the opposite direction from the pack, and the three of us sprinted through the woods.

"We're dead," Charles whimpered. *Dead.*

"There're too many," Yardstick said. "They'll wear us down before long."

Turning to him, I asked, "Any suggestions for plan B?"

"B? Man—we're up to plan Z by now."

I scanned the woods, searching for something, *anything* that might save us.

A lightbulb went off over Yardstick's head. "I know a place."

"Where?"

"Just keep running," he said, picking up the pace. "We're close."

"Close? Close to what?"

An explosion of black feathers burst right in front of me.

*Caw! Caw! Caw!*

Crows—I do believe the appropriate collective noun is a "murder"—scattered into the air. Too many to count. They had been feasting on something, and I stepped directly into their breakfast. Or what was left of it.

The raccoon's decapitated head had been staked to the ground with a tree branch. A cloud of flies swarmed around its face. The crows had pecked out its eyes, leaving behind a pair of hollow sockets wrapped in black fur. Its mouth hung open and its shriveled tongue slung over its lower teeth.

I stepped back. *Lord of the Flies* popped into my head. Something similar had been done with a pig—*The head remained there, dim-eyed, grinning faintly, blood blackening between the teeth.* Guess I wasn't the only one who'd read it recently.

"We're here," Yardstick said.

"Where's *here*?"

"Home."

# CAVE
# SPRAY-PAINTINGS

The opening was five feet wide and looked like a mouth in mid-yawn.

". . . Hello?"

The only response was my voice echoing back.

"Be careful," Yardstick said.

Stirring. Someone was moving, coming closer. I brandished My Little Friend like a canister of pepper spray.

"I heard something," I said. "Is somebody in there?"

"Don't," Yardstick tried to pull me back. "There are—"

Too late. A colony of screeching wings flooded past my face.

Bats. So many bats. It felt like I'd been swept up in a hurricane of wings. Once they flapped by, I made sure there weren't any crawling up my shorts.

"A little warning would've been nice!"

"I tried, didn't I? But you had to go off all half-cocked—"

"Are they gone?" Charles asked, his eyes still pinched tight.

"Looks that way."

Peaking into the cavern, something caught my eye.

Scrawled along the wall of the rocky entrance was the Tribe's stick figure.

So this was where Peashooter had been hiding all this time. . . .

Tribal HQ.

• • •

The air inside was cooler. Shadows clung to the limestone walls. It was impossible to tell how deep the cavern went. A dripping sound echoed through the hollow chasm—*plink, plink, plink*—like a dozen faucets leaking all around us.

Yardstick retrieved a box of strike-anywhere matches and went about lighting candles wedged into a few of the cave's corners.

*Let there be light. . . .*

Before long, a dim glow illuminated a library for the dead.

Piles upon piles of abandoned books surrounded us. Some were fifty-editions tall, looking like literary stalagmites. Mountains of moldy novels, mildewed dictionaries, and yellowed pillars of paperbacks as far as I could see. The cave's damp air had seeped into the paper, making the pages ripple.

The Tribe really had become bookworms.

This had been their home.

I picked up a copy of *Walden*. Inside the front cover, someone had written:

*Jason Bowden*

Flipping through, I stopped on an underlined passage: *The savage in man is never quite eradicated.*

*You got that one right, Mr. Thoreau.*

I found lawn chairs, musty-smelling blankets, pillows without pillowcases, a wheelbarrow filled with batteries, milk crates full of empty bottles, tattered sleeping bags, fishing poles, a pile of radios, a clothesline made of fishing line.

"Where did you get all of this stuff?"

"Some we stole from campsites," Yardstick explained. "The books are all Peashooter's personal collection. The rest we just found. You'd be amazed at what people leave behind out here in the woods."

I picked up a rake from a pile of gardening tools. Its tines were replaced with rusty nails. "Like this?"

"Everybody's got to have a hobby," Yardstick said. "Turns out one of Sporkboy's is making weapons."

"Check out the cave drawings!" Charles marveled, his neck bent back.

"Those aren't drawings," I said, astonished. "That's my yearbook. . . ."

The walls of the cave had been wallpapered with torn pages

from Greenfield Middle's most recent yearbook. So many familiar faces—Martin Mendleson, Riley Callahan, and Sarah Haversand, along with everyone else from school—smiled down at us. Only now, the eyes were crossed out.

When I came across my own photo, I wasn't surprised to find the red rings of a large bull's-eye spray-painted around my head. My grinning mug was dead center.

"These guys really have it out for you," Charles said, amazed.

"I seem to have that effect on a lot of people."

Scrounging around, I found a stack of first-aid kits and tended to Charles's leg as best I could. "Sorry to get you into this mess."

"You kidding? This summer's been the best. Much better than last year."

"Do you think we can get word to your family about tomorrow? Warn them and the rest about Parents' Day?"

"My parents aren't coming." He shrugged. "They never come to Parents' Day."

"And I guess there aren't any cell phones around here, either?" I asked Yardstick.

"None that work," he called out.

I spotted a map of the county plastered to a cave wall. Leaning in for a closer look, I noticed a dot marking my dad's house. Another map detailed an expanse of wooded territory with a circle marking Camp New Leaf.

A pamphlet for the camp hung next to the map. The start date of our session had been circled several times.

Peashooter had counted down the days with a series of slashes on the wall. For every fourth mark, there was a cross through and they'd start another set.

I counted thirty-six sets of marks. A hundred and eighty slashes.

Six months.

*Now, that's what I call patience. . . .*

A copy of Sully's missing flyer was taped to the wall. I pulled it down and folded it, slipping it into my pocket. Peashooter had taken mine, so I'd take his.

An ivy of graffiti stretched along the walls. *I never found a companion that was so companionable as solitude,* was written over the length of the cave's ceiling.

"Let me guess," I asked. "Thoreau?"

Yardstick nodded.

I noticed a batch of photos clustered together along the far corner of the cave. A handful of candles had been stacked around the snapshots, their wicks burnt to the bottom, the wax having long-since hardened across the cavern floor. A shrine.

I crouched down for a better look.

"Don't—" Yardstick started.

They were family photos of Yardstick and his mother. Yardstick wore a tuxedo too small for his frame, his gangly arms reaching out from the sleeves.

There was a photo of a much younger Sporkboy roughhousing with a man who must've been his dad. The two were mugging mid-wrestle.

Looking at those photos, I couldn't help but miss my mom and dad. I remembered when I used to wrestle with my father.

I saw Sully as a little girl at Christmas, sitting with her mom. She couldn't have been any older than ten.

I pulled a photo off the wall. An awkward-looking boy stood beside a woman who must have been his mother and glared directly at the camera. The woman's arm was wrapped around his shoulder. The boy had a cowlick sticking straight up at the back of his head. He had the exact same piercing stare as Peashooter, same icy gray eyes. He was just a kid in the picture, but I was positive it was him.

Flipping it over, I read an inscription someone had hand-written along the back—*Jason, 11 yrs old, and me.*

Yardstick leaned over and removed the picture of himself and his mother.

"Miss her?" I asked.

Staring at the photo, he murmured back, "Every day." He slipped the picture into his pocket and cleared his throat as he walked away.

Charles broke the silence. "Uh—guys? What're we gonna do now?"

"All the campers' families are going to walk right into Peashooter's hands tomorrow if we don't figure out how to stop him."

"There's no way," Yardstick said. "There's only three of us. You can't expect him to go out there and fight." He pointed to Charles.

"Yeah," Charles chimed in. "You can't expect me to go out there!"

"Fine," I said. "Just you and me."

"*Two against twenty?* That's a good way to get ourselves killed."

"What's your plan? Hunker down until everything blows over?"

"I can't go back there." Yardstick shook his head. "Sorry—I just can't."

"Then I'll go myself."

"Then you're crazier than I thought."

"My mom and dad are coming," I explained. "I can't let them waltz into a trap."

"What do you care about what happens to your parents? They sold you out, didn't they?" Yardstick sounded sincere. "You've got a chance to go your own way—and you're gonna muck that up by trying to save the same mom and dad who sent you up the river? The same mom and dad who couldn't care less where you lived, or what medication fried your brain, or whether you lived or died out here in these woods? *That mom and dad?*"

"Yeah." I nodded. "Those are the ones."

I kept flipping the photograph of little Peashooter Jr. over in my hands, reading and re-reading the inscription along the back. I stared Sweet Pea down, standing sullenly just next to his mom, almost as if I expected him to say something.

*What're you looking at?*

Then inspiration hit.

# Part IV: Taking Back the Camp

*Mystify, mislead, and surprise the enemy.*
—Stonewall Jackson

# THIS MEANS WAR

The plan had been to break into George's office.

"That's it?" Yardstick had asked before he and Charles bid me *happy infiltrating*. "That's your master plan?"

"There's a little more to it—but in a nutshell, yeah."

The two of them wished me luck at the mouth of the cave, though the tone of their voices, made it sound like they were figuring out what to wear to my funeral.

"If I'm not back in a couple hours," I said, "maybe it'd be wise for you guys to hitchhike up to Canada. . . ."

"If Peashooter doesn't find us first," Yardstick said.

"Stop worrying so much, will you? It's time to throw a little *civil disobedience* into the mix."

• • •

In less than an hour, a cavalcade of station wagons, sedans, and minivans would pull into the parking lot. Dozens of unsuspecting

261

parents would spill from their cars into camp, where the Tribe would be waiting for them with open arms.

*And hedge clippers.*

The towering pines offered enough cover for me to sneak in to New Leaf without drawing any attention my way.

I stopped at the tree line along the edge of the campground. I waited until I was positive the coast was clear. I took a deep breath, ready to set foot back into camp—when I heard a branch snap. Someone was behind me.

Spinning around, I found Charles plopped in a wheelbarrow. Yardstick had pushed him all the way through the woods behind my back, and I hadn't even noticed.

The breath in my lungs sputtered out. "Don't sneak up on me like that."

"Sorry," Charles said.

"Thought you guys were sitting this one out."

"We couldn't let you have all the glory, could we?" Yardstick asked.

"Why the change of heart?"

"Jaws was getting on my nerves."

"Caves make me claustrophobic," Charles said. "Let me be a lookout."

"Fine by me," I started. "But listen. This is important. If I die today . . ."

Yardstick held up both hands. "Come on, man."

"Let me finish," I said. "If I die today, would you . . . Would you tell my parents I tried. Tell them I know I've been a real pain in the ass, and I know I only made matters worse, and there's no way they could trust me, but that I love them. And that's all that matters."

Yardstick and Charles just stared.

"I'd do the same for you! One of us is bound to get an arrow through the chest today. Or a spear in the neck."

Yardstick let out a laugh. "Or a weed whacker to the crotch."

"Or a rake to the face."

"Or a machete to the mouth," Charles added.

"Or a shovel to the shin," I said.

"Or a pair of hedge clippers to the . . ." Yardstick cut himself off and ducked. He gripped my collar and pulled me behind the tree just as three cannibals passed.

"Looks like everybody's heading to the amphitheater," Charles whispered.

The Piranhas had scampered into the parking lot carrying a bedsheet scrawled with words. They suspended their brand-new banner from the trees:

# WELCOME TO CAMP CANNIBAL, PARENTS!

The ol' stars and stripes was taken down. In its place, they raised a flag made out of a sleeping bag with the silhouette of the Tribe's stick figure stitched against the circle of a full moon, cut from a cotton sheet.

Scanning the grounds, I spotted a squad of cannibals standing guard on top of cabin two's roof.

"Guess that means breaking George and the rest out is a no-go," I whispered. "Think we can sneak into his office without anybody noticing?"

"And do what, exactly?" Yardstick whispered back. "Check your e-mail?"

"I work better when I improvise. Besides, we've got the element of surprise on our side."

"The element of surprise only works when the people doing the surprising *have an actual plan*. I don't want to be just as surprised as the people we're supposed to be surprising. . . ."

"I think better on my feet. Just help me get to the admin cabin, okay?"

"Fine." Yardstick shook his head. "You first."

"Thanks." I stepped out from the tree line. "Here goes nothing."

*Run, run, run*—the broken record kept repeating in my head.

I reached the side of the main cabin just as Compass stepped out the front door.

*Hide, hide, hide*—the broken record skipped a beat in my brain.

I pressed my back against the cabin. Compass turned onto the path and headed for the amphitheater, while I did my best to blend in with the log cabin.

*Don't breathe, don't breathe, don't breathe . . .*

Compass never looked back. I slid along the cabin wall, turned the corner, and rushed for the front door.

*Unlocked.*

George's office had been left unattended. I tiptoed over to his desk and sat before the camp's computer. As soon as I touched the mouse, the monitor lit up like a lightning bug.

Keyword search: *Jack Cumberland.*

*Benjamin Greenwood.*

*Jimmy Winters.*

*Sully Tulliver.*

And the cherry on top . . .

*Jason Bowden.*

I found an online database for missing children. A quick cross-reference with a local telephone directory gave me the names of parents.

Their e-mail addresses.

I pounded the keys as quickly as I could. No time for spell-checking.

A whistle cut through the silence. It sounded like it came from the amphitheater.

I bit my lip as I pressed SEND.

• • •

Yardstick peered out from behind the cabin's side as soon as I slipped out the front door. "Did you pull off your master plan?"

"Only time will tell."

"Sure hope it works," he said. "You're gonna want to see this."

We kept to the outskirts of camp, weaving through the surrounding trees. The perimeter of pines gave us enough cover to pass the cabins undetected and make our way to the rear of the amphitheater.

I peered out from behind a pine, taking in the sight of an army assembling around the fire pit below.

Peashooter stood atop the lifeguard's chair. In his hand, he held a sawed-off broomstick with the bleached skull of a buck mounted on top. Its antlers branched out from the bone like a pair of wings. He had pilfered a quiver full of arrows from the archery range, which rattled at his back.

Thin wisps of smoke escaped from the embers of the bonfire. That fire had chewed through our clothes, our electronics, our personal possessions.

All were nothing but ash now.

"Come and dip your hand into the ashes," Peashooter called out. "It's time we show our true faces."

Cannibals lined up before the bonfire. Klepto was first, his face bruised purple from his little run-in with the Tribe's rock trap yesterday. He reached into the ashes and brought back a blackened hand. He ringed his eyes in soot. He drew a strip of ash down the length of his nose. His darkened eyes looked like two black holes that had swallowed up the boy who'd once gone by the name of Thomas.

"This is a declaration of war," Peashooter shouted as one cannibal after another painted his face. "Let it be known that on this day, brothers, we took a stand against the people who manacled our minds. Against those who abandoned us with love as their excuse."

More and more cannibals completed their ashen transformation. Their faces now looked like skulls.

"Who is our enemy? Those who believe they know better— *but know nothing about us at all.*"

Sporkboy distributed his artillery of weaponized gardening equipment amongst the cannibals. Hoes bound together and sharpened into double-headed battle axes. Hedge clippers that had been separated in half for dual-purpose machete action. Handmade flails made from handheld rototillers.

The campers looked like gardeners of the apocalypse.

"What is matriphagy?" Peashooter asked the assembly.

Compass knew the answer, and he shouted it out. "The condition where organisms feed on their own mother."

"Exactly." Peashooter beamed. "Spiders do it the second they hatch, and now you will too. Because you are reborn! You are now all cannibals! And it is time to sever the ties that bind. Break them with your own teeth!"

I glanced back at Yardstick. He only shook his head in disbelief.

Peashooter was out for blood.

"Look around you," Peashooter continued. "Your true colors are shining now, bright and blinding. I see them—and they are glorious! Your families should be afraid!"

Sporkboy had taken a pair of hand cultivators, those three-tined hand forks used for breaking up soil, and strapped them to his wrists with duct tape.

Instant claws. He raised his forked-fists into the air, shouting—"To the Law of Claw and Fang!"

"This is our home," Peashooter cried as he raised his arms. "And today, the war comes to our front door!"

Compass pierced the air above his head with his compass-pinkie—"Claw and Fang!"

The campers joined in—"Claw and Fang!"

"Claw and Fang!"

"Claw and Fang!"

"This is not Parents' Day," he roared. "This is *your* day! And by the time the sun sets, you will be emancipated from your families once and for all!"

"Claw and Fang!"

"Claw and Fang!"

"Claw and Fang!"

Peashooter scanned his chanting army like a proud father. There was an unbridled wildness in their eyes. Nothing could stop them now.

The Piranhas rushed into the amphitheater, leaping up and down and shouting at the top of their lungs—

"Theyarehereourparentsarecomingourparentsarecoming theyarehere!"

Right on schedule.

Time for war.

Our families didn't stand a chance.

# THE PARENTAL PROCESSIONAL OF LEMMINGS

I motioned toward the amphitheater for us to move in, but Yardstick vigorously shook his head. He mouthed out a silent *no* just in case I couldn't comprehend his apprehension.

I widened my eyes to express my own emphatic attitude, but Yardstick hooked his arm around my chest and started dragging me deeper into the woods, away from the action in the amphitheater.

"What are you doing?" I whispered.

"Too many of them."

"We can at least try and cut the cars off." I couldn't squirm free from Yardstick's grip. "We can tell them to turn around and get help!"

Yardstick froze. His arm slackened around me as he stared off into the distance. "Too late."

I followed his gaze to a minivan turning into the parking lot.

A station wagon was close on its tail, followed by another car. Then another.

I bolted for the parking lot.

"*Don't,*" Yardstick whisper-hissed, chasing after.

Moms and dads climbed out from their cars, greeted by the serene sight of a calm campground. Everything was eerily quiet. Just the billowing of the Tribe's flag in the breeze. The sun shone from overhead, its warm rays reaching through the trees, while a pair of birds lovingly chirped from somewhere off in the distance.

What could possibly be wrong with this picture?

One father called out, "Hello . . . ?"

No answer. No welcoming committee.

"Anyone?" He tried again.

I scanned the crowd of parents, looking for a familiar face. Nothing.

*Maybe my parents are stuck in traffic.*

Whatever it was, I was thankful they were running late.

A bloodred arrow pointed the adults toward the amphitheater, funneling them onto the path that bottlenecked between the cabins. They chatted amicably as they walked in pairs. None of these parents knew each other, but they all knew what it's like to raise a kid who constantly burned things and stole stuff and lied about everything.

I stepped forward, my mouth opening. "Stay ba—"

I felt a foot plant itself directly in the small of my back, drop-kicked from behind. My whole body was flung forward, until I face-planted into a patch of leaves.

Before I could pick myself up, Yardstick was pinning me to the ground.

I spat out a mouthful of dirt. "I have to stop them before—"

"*Look.*" Yardstick pointed up ahead. "Cabin one."

Firefly and Klepto were on the roof. Klepto was armed with his bow and arrow while Firefly brandished a bag of . . .

"Wait." I squinted. "What is that?"

Firefly reached into the bag and crammed something into his mouth. Before long, he looked like a chipmunk, his cheeks ballooning out. He spat out a slimy white cannonball into his palm and pierced the gooey ball onto the tip of Klepto's arrow.

"I could be wrong," Yardstick said, "but that sure looks like marshmallow ammunition to me."

"That's just disgusting."

Klepto slid the bulbous-tipped arrow into his bow—*locked and loaded.*

"Ready," I could see Klepto's lips mouth out the command.

Firefly pulled out a canister of—*I do believe that's lighter fluid*—from his pocket and doused the marshmallow mush.

"Aim . . ."

Klepto pulled the bow's string back and pinpointed his target. Firefly struck a match and the wad burst into brilliant flames.

"*Fire!*"

Klepto sent the arrow streaking through the air. It arced

over the heads of every unsuspecting parent below and stuck itself to the front tire of the closest minivan.

*Bull's-eye.* Marshmallow napalm. *Impressive.*

Firefly spat out another marshmallow projectile.

Klepto reloaded his bow.

Firefly lit the marshmallow tip, and off the arrow went— this time striking the tire of a station wagon. Their tires were now on fire, a toxic cloud of black smoke billowing upward. The noxious odor of burning rubber mixed with sugar permeated the atmosphere. Parents started to cough, choking on the sweet smoke.

"Too late to help them now." Yardstick rolled off and lay beside me. "Here comes phase two. . . ."

Parents had been too distracted by the blockade of burning automobiles to notice the swarm of campers rising up along the rooftops of each cabin. One father took a step toward the parking lot, only for a burning bottle to smash at his feet.

*CRASH!*

The glass shattered. A thin blanket of fire sprawled across the path. The father leapt back, kicking a bud of flames off from the tip of his left shoe.

Another bottle burst over the footpath.

*CRASH!*

Looking up, parents discovered a line of half-naked campers, chests streaked in soot. Each pitched their own glass soda-bottle Molotov cocktail onto the ground.

*CRASH!*

*CRASH!*

*CRASH!*

One mother screamed. Like a herd of cattle, the throng of adults stampeded toward the amphitheater.

"What time is it?" I asked Yardstick.

"Does it look like I'm wearing a watch?" he shot back. "Who cares what time it is anyway?"

"Where are they?"

"Where's *who?*"

"The cavalry," I said. "We've got to move."

This time, he didn't stop me.

The Tribe was so focused on corralling our families, none even thought to look over their own shoulders. That gave me the perfect opportunity to reach the perimeter of the amphitheater without drawing attention my way.

I glanced back and realized Yardstick hadn't followed me. I couldn't find him anywhere.

I was on my own.

Nobody noticed my best guerrilla-gorilla routine as I scrambled up a nearby pine and shimmied onto an overhanging branch directly above the fire pit.

*Hope nobody looks up.*

Parents flooded into the amphitheater and skidded to a halt. There was nowhere for the frantic herd of husbands and wives to go.

Perched upon the inner circle of logs were our counselors, wearing the tattered rags of their New Leaf T-shirts. Each wore a baseball cap with the rim low, hiding their eyes. They sat stock-still, some slumped over each other, focusing their attention on the ashen remains of the bonfire.

"Thank God you're here," one particularly jittery mother blurted as she reached her hand out to grab the nearest counselor. "We thought you—"

The moment she clutched the counselor's shoulder, his head rolled off.

That decapitated head landed on the ground and burst apart. Bits of straw scattered over this mother's high-heeled feet as she screamed and screamed.

Scarecrows.

Another mother froze. "Look!"

Cannibals now surrounded the entire border of the amphitheater, their wild faces smeared with ash. They pounded their bare soot-streaked chests and howled.

"Thomas, is that . . . ?" one father started.

"Jonathan—what's going on?" another asked.

"Edward, please—"

At the sound of their old names, each cannibal raised their weapon over his head and shrieked. These names were murder to their ears. A mother clasped her hands over her head as the Tribe's battle cry echoed into the woods.

Then—silence.

Chests heaved as the circle of cannibals opened to allow

Peashooter to pass. The crown of deer antlers perched upon his head made him look like the devil.

"Welcome. We've been expecting you."

"Just what on God's green earth is going on here?" a dad demanded with a bullheaded obliviousness. "What's come over you kids? Where are the counselors?"

"Hear that?" Peashooter laughed. "Mommy and Daddy want to know what's going on here!"

The Tribe's snickering filled the amphitheater like a pack of hyenas howling over carrion. Peashooter lifted his skull quarter-staff into the air, silencing the Tribe.

*"All men recognize the right of revolution,"* Peashooter pronounced, personalizing Thoreau. *"That is, the right to refuse allegiance to, and to resist* our parents *when their tyranny or their inefficiency are great and unendurable."*

A chorus of shouts rose up.

Most moms and dads stepped back. As I watched their faces, I could see it dawn on some of them just how dire their situation was, while others stubbornly refused to believe their eyes.

"What is this?" the oblivious father kept persisting. He scanned the crowd until he locked onto Klepto. "Thomas—just what do you think you're doing?"

Klepto didn't say a word. He held up his chin and clenched his bow.

"Thomas, please," his mother started. "Just tell us where the adults are?"

Ever watch a clueless grown-up attempt to regain control of

a group of wild children? They always try reason. They hide behind a protective blanket of their own logic. They demand explanations, insisting that they are right, that they deserve respect—that just because they're older, they're in control.

I couldn't help but cringe.

"No adults here," Peashooter said. "We are the ones in control now."

"Mason." Another dad took a step forward, hands planted on his hips. "You want to explain to me what this is all about?"

"Keep the fire burning at all times!" Firefly shouted. "Gotta feed the flames!"

"We don't have to explain anything to you anymore." Peashooter spoke on Firefly's behalf, and for all the members of Camp Cannibal.

"Is that so?" Firefly's father huffed. "And who are you supposed to be, kid?"

Peashooter remained calm. "I am everything you prayed would never come to pass. I am the inevitable. I am the future. I am . . ."

Peashooter paused.

"I am the father of these kids now."

Peashooter swept his deer-skulled quarterstaff across the back of the man's leg, striking him in the soft of his knee joint.

Firefly's father folded over on his knees.

Two other fathers stepped forward, ready to come to this man's aid—but before they could reach him, the Tribe readied their weapons. Both men froze.

"You all must be parched from such a long journey," Peashooter said. "We thought we might offer you some refreshments to quench your thirst."

Sporkboy entered the amphitheater holding a tray full of paper cups. Each miniature paper cup was full of bright-orange liquid.

"Line up," Sporkboy announced. "Time to *drink the Kool-Aid*."

I scanned the crowd and found Klepto. His tackle box was by his feet. If I were a betting boy, I had a pretty good guess at the cocktail of prescription meds in those refreshments.

Peashooter turned to Firefly's father. "You first, sir."

It didn't sound like he had much choice in the matter.

Firefly's father picked up a cup from the tray. He brought it up to his mouth, then hesitated. He looked to his son. "Mason . . . ?" The name died as it left his mouth.

"My name is Firefly now."

Firefly's father looked down at the cup in his hand.

"Down the hatch," Peashooter said.

*Do something, Spencer. Stop this.*

Firefly's father brought the cup to his lips.

*Now!*

I closed my eyes. And let go of the branch.

I felt like I was flying.

Until I landed on top of Firefly's dad. The paper cup tumbled out from his hand as we both splatted on the ground.

"Sorry to drop in like this," I said, struggling to stand.

Klepto was quick to hit me upside the head with his tackle box. A hailstorm of pills showered over the ground.

Peashooter snatched a cup from Sporkboy's tray. With his free hand, he clutched my lower jaw and squeezed until my lips puckered.

"Don't worry, Rat," he muttered, fuming. "You're just in time."

Peashooter raised the cup over his head.

"A toast! To Spencer Pendleton." Peashooter brought the cup to my mouth. "May you rest in peace. . . ."

I tried to wriggle my lips free from his fingers and seal them shut, but his grip around my jaw was too tight.

*"Bottoms up."*

Kool-Aid suddenly exploded everywhere. The cup seemed to burst all on its own. My face was dripping wet while Peashooter held the shreds of a paper cup.

"Hey, Peashooter!" A lone voice cut through the amphitheater.

All heads turned.

*Sully?*

She stood at the rear with her slingshot pulled taut, aiming right at Peashooter. Her hair, her never-ending hair, was now braided into tight cornrows that wove around her scalp in a spiral pattern, like a conch shell.

"Can the boys come out and play?"

She pivoted on her heels and fired. Rather than hit Peashooter, Sporkboy got a rock right in the wrist. His hand slackened and dropped the tray.

Paper cups crashed at his feet. A wave of florescent-orange Kool-Aid washed over the ground before soaking into the soil.

Sully cricked her neck back until she was facing the sky. Taking in a deep breath, she let out a high-pitched ululation:

"*Lalalalalalalala!*"

One second, they weren't there. The next, they leapt out from perched positions over our heads.

They must have been hiding in the trees all along. Now, like ripe fruit falling from a branch, they dropped into the amphitheater.

*How could I not have noticed them?*

Each girl had their hair done up in a different style. Spirals of black cornrows, a brown ponytail halo braided around the scalp, blond Bantu knots, red Celtic lassos, all swirled around their heads in order to keep their hair out of their fiercely ornamented faces. Red stripes lined their noses. Blue dots freckled their cheeks. Yellow swirls surrounded their eyes. Green bolts lashed over their foreheads.

Before one boy could raise his weapon, the horizon was eclipsed with a circle of girls, their tongues lashing at the roofs of their mouths, echoing Sully's battle cry.

"*Lalalalalalalala!*"

# THE BATTLE OF CAMP CANNIBAL

Let it be known that on this sunny morning, on the eighth day of summer camp, at eleven a.m., Camp Cannibal became a battlefield.

There will come a day when kids all across the country will turn to one another in the cafeteria and ask—*Where were you on that fateful summer morning?*

A select few will roll up their sleeves and show channels of raised flesh as living proof of who fought on that fated day.

*I was there*, they will say. *It was one for the history books.*

• • •

Just across Lake Wendigo, the female faction of Camp New Leaf had been keeping themselves very, *very* busy.

While the boys had been occupying their time by torturning

me, Sully had trained her fellow campers in marksmanship and military tactics.

Not to mention battlefield accessorizing.

Each girl wielded her own handmade slingshot, plus a fanny pack loaded with rocks and a florescent-yellow jump rope coiled at her waist.

Klepto was the first to break from the front line. There were only three steps between him and the amphitheater's entrance when Sully grabbed the rope at her hip. The yellow spool unraveled as she spun it over her head and released.

The loop twirled through the air before swallowing Klepto at his shoulders.

"Where are you going?" She gave a yank, sending him to the ground. "The fun's just started."

I spotted the blonde from the other night, her hair still braided to the side of her head. She looked up to the sky with the rest and flicked her tongue across her teeth.

"*Lalalalalalalalala!*"

They wore the same red shorts and white T-shirts. In puffy red iron-on letters, it read NEW LEAF across the front, along with the maple-leafed moose head. The seams along their shoulders were lined in white goose feathers, like wings. Strapped to their chests were two Popsicle sticks glued into an *X*, wrapped in multicolored yarn.

The Tribe had their insignia, and Sully's crew had their crest. She had struck out on her own.

This was her Tribe.

Not Peashooter's.

"Take them down!" he shouted as he scaled his lifeguard chair. He hovered above the skirmish, calling out orders. "Don't be afraid of fighting back because they're girls! This is the fight we've been preparing for all summer! This is your—"

He raised a fist into the air, a breath away from sounding his own battle cry.

As soon as his mouth opened, he choked.

Clutching his throat, Peashooter spat out a rock with a couple teeth.

I spun back to Sully to see her slingshot still held up in the air. She spotted me from across the amphitheater and winked.

Compass rushed up to the choking Peashooter and helped him down from the lifeguard chair, yelling—*"Attaaaaaaaack!"*

The command was given.

Time to fight.

But instead of the boys going after their parents, they charged the girls.

Sully sounded her battle cry. *"Lalalalalalala!"*

The ululation passed from mouth to mouth.

*"Lalalalalalalalala!"*

Each girl pinpointed a target, and together they released a hailstorm of rocks.

"Aim for the soft spots," Sully ordered. "Incapacitate and disarm!"

They targeted wrists.

Ankles.

Knees.

Even the groin. Anything to relieve these boys of their weaponized gardening tools and get them down on the ground.

I seized the moment to usher panicking parents away from the crossfire. It must've looked like the most brutal game of capture the flag ever.

Husbands hugged their wives and crouched down low to avoid the firefight between these two warring tribes.

"Stay down," I shouted over the commotion.

Thomas's father absentmindedly nodded, shell-shocked. "What is this?"

"This? Just our annual Camp New Leaf Olympiad. You know—egg tosses, three-legged races, head-hunting. Standard summer stuff. *Very* therapeutic."

I looked up and realized Peashooter was no longer in his high chair. Compass was attempting to pull him out of the amphitheater, but Peashooter refused to abandon their cannibalistic comrades as they rolled around the ground, clutching their knees.

"We need to evacuate," Compass shouted.

Peashooter pulled free from his grip. "Don't tell me to give up!"

"We've already lost!"

Compass was right. The girls had laid down a steady

bombardment of slingshot fire, taking the bulk of the boys to the ground. Once they were down, the girls pounced and tethered them up with their jump ropes so no one could run.

*Incapacitate.*

*Detain.*

*Repeat.*

Suddenly there were more boys rocking and moaning on the ground than on their feet.

When the remaining cannibals realized they were outnumbered, that they couldn't win against the girls—the strangest thing happened. Something neither myself nor Peashooter or anyone else could ever have anticipated.

The boys turned against the camp.

Taking whatever they could grab off the ground—whether it was their handmade weapon or a rock or a branch—the pack of feral campers rushed through New Leaf to wreak whatever destruction they were still capable of.

Cabin windows shattered.

The lifeguard chair was pushed over into the fire pit.

A hay bale from the archery range was lit on fire. I jumped out of the way just in time to dodge the flaming bundle as it smashed into the lifeguard chair, sending burning bits of hay into the air.

Parents screamed, running in every direction.

"What's wrong with you?" Peashooter shouted. "What are you doing? *This is your home! You're destroying your own home!*"

Peashooter couldn't stop them. He'd lost control of his own Tribe. I watched him search the crowd. When he spotted Sully, he summoned all the bilious spite he could muster and pointed—"*You.*"

He charged. Sully lifted her slingshot, ready to reload, but Peashooter was upon her before she could fire, knocking it out of her hand.

"Sully!" I was halfway to the rescue when a fibrously fluffy tennis ball consumed with flame crashed at my feet.

Then another.

Looking up, I saw Firefly now perched on the roof to cabin four. He had a tennis racket and over a dozen tennis balls. Using a pair of tongs from the mess hall, he dipped each ball into a bucket of gasoline, lit it on fire—and *served.*

Blazing tennis balls volleyed through the air.

"*Feed the flames,*" Firefly screeched as he wantonly lobbed balls into the sky with no regard to where they landed. He could care less what his target was. "*Feed the flames, feed the flames!*"

"The fires," I shouted, stomping on a burning ball. "Put out the fires!"

Sporkboy popped up out of nowhere and pushed me to the ground.

"Stop being such a spoilsport," he said as he reeled back, ready to belly flop.

I shrank into myself as Sporkboy closed in. His feet were about to leap off the ground—when, right over his shoulder, I sighted Charles barreling down the amphitheater's path in his wheelbarrow, Yardstick steering straight for us.

"Incoming!" Charles yelled.

Sporkboy turned just in time to see Yardstick dig his heels in. The sudden halt propelled Charles from the wheelbarrow arcing through the air.

*A cannibal catapult.*

Charles unlocked his mandibles.

The steel trap of his lower jaw swung open.

The second Charles pounced upon Sporkboy, his teeth sank into the soft flesh of Sporkboy's throat and clamped down.

The two hit the ground, rolling over each other. Their bodies eventually stopped with Charles on top, pinning Sporkboy to the ground by his mouth.

Charles growled, keeping his teeth clamped onto Sporkboy's neck flesh.

Sporkboy's eyes lolled over to one side and settled upon Yardstick, while the rest of his body remained extremely still.

"You're picking Spencer over us?" he asked. "Your own family?"

"My family wouldn't do this."

I stepped over Sporkboy and stood next to Yardstick. "I thought you bolted."

"Just doing a little improvising."

"You okay down there?" I asked Charles.

"Na pwowem. Ah gaht wis cwovured."

Most girls watched on in bewilderment as the remaining

cannibals ransacked their own camp. Rather than fight, they dismantled the cabin doors and flung them through the windows. They ripped shingles off rooftops with their bare hands.

"Claw and Fang!"

"Claw and Fang!"

"Claw and Fang!"

Flaming tennis balls continued to rain down. One landed on the roof of cabin three and rolled into the gutter. Before long, smoke spirited into the air.

"Let me deal with Firefly," Yardstick said. "You take care of Peashooter."

*Where was he?*

I scanned the chaos but couldn't find him or Sully anywhere.

*They had just been here a second ago. . . .*

Compass wandered aimlessly through the amphitheater. "Stop," he implored. "All of you—*stop!*"

Several cannibals pushed the logs out from their original position within the amphitheater's circle and watched them barrel down the slope. Several parents had to leap out of the way before the tumbling tree trunks crashed into the fire pit.

"Claw and Fang!"

"Claw and Fang!"

"Claw and Fang!"

"Peashooter gave you your freedom," Compass continued, his pleas falling on deaf ears. "He gave you everything you ever—"

A blur of tiny limbs quickly enveloped him.

*The Piranhas!*

The pack of hyperactive campers latched on to his legs and arms, then sank their teeth into whatever piece of Compass was closest—his thigh, his bicep, his shoulder.

"Timetoeattimetoeatdinnerbellisringingyumyummyinour tummy . . ."

One Piranha climbed onto his back and wrapped his hands around Compass's eyes. Before he could yank the hands away, that Piranha sank his teeth into his ear.

"Get off of me!" Compass shrieked. "Get off—"

"Rubadubdubthanksforthegrubrubadubdubthanksforthe grub . . ."

The Piranhas wrapped around his legs, grabbed one another and pulled, cinching Compass at the knees. He toppled to the ground, howling from underneath the pile of tiny bodies. He lashed frantically—but it was useless.

A Piranha looked up at me and grinned, blood smeared across his teeth.

"*Bon appétit*," I said and stepped back. I could hear Compass from below, screaming—"Get them off, get them off, *get them oooooooff.*"

I raced out from the amphitheater, surveying the mayhem for Peashooter and Sully.

The cabins had been scavenged, and windows smashed. Farther down the path, several cannibals took to the parking lot. They hopped onto their parents' cars and a cacophony of car alarms and shattered glass rang out into the air.

"Claw and Fang!"

"Claw and Fang!"

"Claw and Fang!"

But this wasn't the Law of Claw and Fang. Not the way Peashooter had imagined.

This was chaos.

Utter anarchy.

Smoke was rising up from the roofs of several cabins now, growing thicker and highlighted by flashes of yellow.

Camp New Leaf was burning.

Peashooter gave his cannibals permission to burn the world down. Now he had no choice but to stand upon the scorched earth and watch his master plan crumble.

If I could just find him.

I zeroed in on the docks. Found them. Peashooter had cornered Sully at the end. Her bare heels were inching toward the edge, while his back was turned to me.

Another inch and she'd be bathing in Lake Wendigo.

My feet were in flight before the rest of me knew what I was doing. I rushed onto the dock, trying not to make a sound. The wood warped beneath my feet.

Sully's eyes left Peashooter long enough to lock on to mine.

*Instant giveaway.*

Peashooter spun around and slipped behind Sully, wrapping his arm around her neck.

My feet skidded to a halt, my fist withering at my side.

"Hello, *Rat*," Peashooter purred. "I was starting to think you'd never make it."

"Wouldn't miss this for the world."

Sully tried to free herself from his grip. "Spencer—*don't*. He's mine."

"Good to see you, too," I said. "Nice of you to drop in and pay a visit."

"Well, I was in the neighborhood."

"Shall we end this?" I asked, taking a step forward. Peashooter's arm tightened around Sully's throat like a boa constrictor coiling around its prey.

"Let her go," I said. "This is between you and me."

"Isn't that sweet," Peashooter whispered in Sully's ear. "Your boyfriend has come to rescue you." He stepped back, the lake shimmering just over his shoulder.

"Him? Rescue *me*?" Sully huffed. "My hero."

"You should be ashamed, Peashooter. Picking on a defenseless girl."

"*Excuse me?*" Sully prickled at my comment. "Just who do you think you're calling *defenseless*?"

"Would you stay out of this, please? I'm trying to save your life!"

"If you two want to hash this out amongst yourselves," Peashooter interrupted, growing impatient, "I'll gladly wait until you're done."

"Stay out of this," I spat back at Peashooter before returning to Sully.

She rolled her eyes at me. "You have no idea how annoying you are sometimes."

"You can say that again," Peashooter agreed.

"Let her go," I said.

"I don't need your help," Sully growled. "This is between Peashooter and me."

"No," I insisted. "This is between me and him."

"This is between all of us," Peashooter said. Without hesitating, he flung Sully off the dock. She hit the surface of the lake with a sharp splash.

"Sully!" I lost sight of her as she sank farther below.

"What are you going to do now that your girlfriend's gone?" he asked.

My fingers balled themselves into a fist. Peashooter grinned.

"Are you going to hit me?"

I could feel my fingernails dig into my skin as I tightened my fist.

"Come on. Take your best shot."

I didn't lift my arm.

"What's the matter? Hit me! *Hit me!*"

Peashooter was only growing more frustrated the longer I held my ground. He picked up his deer-skulled quarterstaff from the dock and trained the antlers on me. I noticed a braided belt of rubber bands strung between them.

"Can't take the first swing? Fine. I'll make you."

*A crossbow.* That was most definitely a crossbow. Peashooter pulled out an arrow from the quiver rattling at his back.

"No more dart guns made out of pens, huh?" I asked.

"I have an arrow with your name on it, Spencer."

*Do something, Spence.*

Peashooter took aim.

*Man up man up man up man up man up man up . . .*

I stood in place.

I took in a deep breath.

I lifted my chin.

I faced Peashooter head-on and recited: *"A man who won't die for something is not fit to live."*

"Whoever said that probably wasn't staring down a loaded crossbow."

"The man who said it knew how to fight back against petty tyrants like you. . . ."

"Oh yeah?" Peashooter pinched one eye shut and took aim. "How's that?"

As he pulled his arm back, a yellow jump rope noosed itself around Peashooter's neck and pulled him backward.

"Collective action," Sully answered.

Peashooter released his crossbow and the arrow shot uselessly into the sky. The quarterstaff clattered against the planks.

A soaking-wet Sully hoisted herself back onto the dock, in the process yanking Peashooter into Lake Wendigo, swapping places with him. He shouted all the way down, then was abruptly cut off the moment he took a header through the water's smooth surface.

"You okay?" I asked.

"You said all those chauvinistic things just to throw Peashooter off and let me do my thing, didn't you?"

"Worked, didn't it?"

I can't quite say that any of this had *exactly* been my plan, but, considering it seemed to have been successful, I wasn't going to split hairs.

● ● ●

It took less than an hour to corral all the cannibals. Sully's tribe went about hog-tying the boys, binding their hands and feet behind their backs with jump rope.

The Piranhas had gone rogue, on nobody's side but their own, leaping from one prostrate boy to the next, plucking the hems of their underwear and yanking—

"Deathbywedgiedeathbywedgiedeathbywedgiedeathbywedgiedeathbywedgie."

The aftermath of battle was strewn all around us. Sully and I surveyed a scene eerily reminiscent of those battlefield photos taken during the Civil War.

Parents wandered through the carnage, looking for their sons.

Yardstick had finally knocked Firefly off the rooftop. The girls filled trash cans with water from Lake Wendigo and lugged them back up the path, extinguishing each blaze they stumbled across.

Plumes of smoke continued to drift up from the cabins, blackening the air.

"This is one Parents' Day these parents won't forget," said Sully.

I stopped.

Sully noticed and turned back. "What is it?"

"I thought you had booked it for good."

"As far as Peashooter was concerned, I had. But somebody needed to save your ass—*again*. This is like the fifth time I've come to your rescue."

"But who's counting, right?"

"You're a real regular damsel in distress, Spencer. You know that?"

Silence. I couldn't help but stare.

Six months. It had been six months since I'd last seen Sully. I had imagined this moment so many times, so many different ways. But in the million-and-one scenarios I conjured up in my head (*Sully showing up at my front door, Sully popping out of my locker, Sully dropping down the chimney*), none of them had looked like this.

"Getting googly-eyed on me already?" she asked, her words punctuated with a slight laugh. Her joke was meant to break the tension, but I couldn't relax.

"Why did you leave?"

The question hung in the air. "We had no choice."

"*You* had a choice."

"I wasn't about to abandon my friends."

"You abandoned *me*."

"You're pretty easy to find."

"So you've been following me?"

"Something like that."

I took Sully's hand. "These last six months were the worst months of my life."

"Spencer . . ."

"I thought you were gone. Gone for good."

Sully leaned in and kissed me. The cicadas grinding away in the woods engulfed the air. I swore I felt the buzzing of their wings in my lips.

Sully stepped back, blinking.

"What?" I asked.

"Usually you'd be having an asthma attack by now."

She was right. But my lungs felt sturdy. As a matter of fact, I hadn't needed My Little Friend for almost twenty-four hours straight.

I took in a lungful of fresh air and slowly exhaled.

No constricted throat.

No dizziness.

Just then, from over Sully's shoulder, I noticed Yardstick racing down the path. His face was painted with an expression of pure panic. "Spencer—*look out!*"

I turned.

There, from the dock, Peashooter took aim with his crossbow.

Time thickened as he pulled the arrow back through the antlers.

Its trajectory seemed off-kilter. The arrow would miss me by a mile.

That's when I realized Peashooter hadn't been aiming for me.

Sully's knees softened. She folded into herself and landed on her back.

"Sully!"

The arrow had buried itself into her shoulder. Her white cotton T-shirt quickly went red, her own blood eclipsing the maple-leafed moose head. The goose feathers lining her shoulders grew crimson, like a pillow fight gone bloody.

*"Did Peashooter just shoot me?"* Sully actually sounded more incredulous than hurt. "I can't believe that jerk just shot me. . . ."

"It's going to be okay," I said, struggling to force the anxiety out of my voice. "Just stay still, alright? Here—hold on to my hand."

"You're not helping."

"Don't—just don't talk. We'll get you to a doc—"

Sully yanked the arrow out with her own hand, her face contorting in pain. A shout seethed out from her gritted teeth.

*"What are you doing?"* I took off my T-shirt and pressed it against her wound. "This badass attitude is a little much, don't you think?"

"Peashooter should stick to his spitballs," she said, and limply laughed. "He's a much better aim with his dart gun."

*Peashooter.*

I turned back to the dock to discover he had reloaded his crossbow.

"To the Law of Claw and Fang," he said, pinching one eye shut.

Ready . . .

Aim . . .

*Good-bye, Spence.*

". . . Jason?"

The name cut through camp.

Nearly everyone seemed to freeze, turning their heads to see who had said it.

A bashful-looking woman stood on the main path, startled by the aftermath of battle spread out before her. Her gray eyes remained on Peashooter.

*Where had she come from?*

She wasn't one of the parents who had been corralled in the amphitheater.

Who she was, nobody knew.

Except for Peashooter. His lower lip began to tremble.

"Mom . . . ?"

# FAMILY REUNION

S o guess who had pressed SEND on an e-mail to the parents of each Tribesman earlier that morning?

> Dear (—————),
>
> This will no doubt come as a shock, but you've got to believe me. . . .
>
> Your son/daughter, (—————), is very much alive—and I know where you can find him/her. THIS IS NOT A PRANK.
>
> My name is Spencer and I'm attending a summer camp in the middle of absolutely nowhere called Camp New Leaf. I don't have any way of proving this, but (—————) is here. He/she is safe—but you've got to hurry. He/she bound to bolt if he/she find out that you're on your way.

No matter how preposterous this sounds,
trust me—if you want to see your son/daughter,
hop in the car and head to New Leaf right
now. . . .

Signed,

Spencer Pendleton

It was hard to tell who was more shocked at the impromptu
reunion—Peashooter or his mother. Both looked as if they'd just
seen a ghost.

"I saw the smoke," Peashooter's mom said, her voice catching
in her throat.

I could immediately see the resemblance between them.
They shared the same eyes. She was the matriarch of the master-
mind behind the Tribe.

And she wasn't alone.

Another pair of parents hurried into the amphitheater. They
looked lost, searching through the crowd of campers for that one
familiar face.

I recognized them from their photos stuck to the cave's walls.

Sporkboy's mom and dad—the Greenwoods.

Charles finally released Sporkboy from his jaws, which had
been clamped down on Sporkboy's throat this whole time, pinning him in place.

Sporkboy sat upright, a ring of teeth marks sunk into his
skin.

"Mom . . . ? Dad?"

His parents remained frozen, speechless.

"It's me, Mom," he said as he stood up and held out his arms at his sides like an infant learning how to walk, struggling to maintain his balance as he took his first few steps toward his mother.

Mrs. Greenwood's mouth opened and closed, but no words came out. Sporkboy stumbled directly into his mother and broke down.

"Can we go home now?" His muffled voice seeped out, face buried in her chest. Mrs. Greenwood lifted her arms and tightly wrapped them around her son.

Mr. Tulliver was the next to arrive at the amphitheater. As soon as Sully saw him, her breath caught in her chest.

"Dad?"

He saw Sully lying on the ground and rushed to her without a second's hesitation, his face a mixture of bliss and panic.

"What happened to you?" he asked. Once the questions started, the dam broke. "Who did this? Are you okay? Where have you been?"

"Dad—I'm fine, I swear."

"We've got to get you to a doctor. We've got to get you out of here. We've got to get you home. We've got to—"

"Dad, please—I'm okay, really."

He picked her up and cradled his daughter against his chest as if she were a newborn. She resisted at first, squirming in his grip.

"I thought . . ." he started to say, choking. "I thought you were dead."

Sully slowly melted into her father's arms. She buried her face into his shoulder and sobbed.

Yardstick's mom—Ms. Cumberland—entered the amphitheater, clutching her purse. Upon first glimpse of her boy—now as tall as a man—she immediately went about fussing over him. She wet her finger with her tongue and attempted to clean the smudges of dirt spread across his forehead.

"Look at you! You look like you haven't taken a bath in years."

"Mom . . . not in front of everybody." Yardstick stood stock-still while she wiped his face, then the two of them fell into each others arms and squeezed.

The Piranhas had scampered off, leaving behind a stunned Compass to stumble above the amphitheater on his own. He nearly collided into his own parents as they entered. The Winters had a much harder time showing their emotions, looking none too happy to be here. His dad possessed a sternness that barely cracked around the corners. He held himself back, arms crossed at his chest.

"Can someone please explain what this is all about?" Mrs. Winters asked.

Before Compass could answer, Mr. Winters cut in. "How could you have done this? To us? Your own parents! Do you know what you put your mother through?"

"*Stanley*," Mrs. Winters admonished her husband. "Not now."

"We're leaving," Mr. Winters declared. "Say good-bye to your friends."

"But . . ." Compass started.

"This instant, Jim. Don't make me say it twice."

"No."

Mr. Winters's features froze. "What did you say to me?"

Compass's hands, clasped in front of him, shook—but he stood his ground. "I said no."

Mr. Winters stormed over to his son. Staring Compass right in the eye, he whispered—"You have three seconds, you hear? Starting now."

Compass took one last look at Peashooter on the docks.

"Three . . ."

Compass turned to Sporkboy, pleading with his eyes.

"Two . . ."

Compass slowly bowed his head.

"One."

Mr. Winters cupped the nape of Compass's neck with his palm, as if to make sure he wouldn't run. The reunited Winters family shuffled up the main path together and disappeared into the smoke-ridden parking lot without another word.

The rest of us just watched Jimmy Winters walk away with his parents.

Compass was gone.

I turned to Peashooter, expecting him to say something. To stop this from happening. Nothing.

Peashooter's mother took an uncertain step out onto the wobbly dock.

"I didn't believe it at first," she said. "After all these years, I—I just couldn't. But I had to come. I needed to see if it was really you." She hesitantly reached out her hand. "Is it? Is it really you . . . ?"

Just as she was about to touch his cheek, Peashooter ran off the dock. His face was wet with tears.

"Jason? Jason, *please*—come back!"

I stepped into Peashooter's path, blocking him. He pushed against me, but I grabbed his arm. I had to dig my heels into the ground just to keep my grip.

"Let go of me!" Peashooter was sobbing.

Actually sobbing.

"Let go!"

His mother followed. "It's okay, baby . . . Everything is going to be okay."

"It's not going to be okay!"

"Jason . . ."

Peashooter's jaw tensed. "Don't call me that. *Nobody* calls me that."

"Jason, please—"

"Jason is dead, you hear me? Jason doesn't exist anymore."

"That's not true. . . ."

"You want to know what happened to your Jason?" Peashooter asked. "Let me remind you. Jason never met his father. His *real* father. For the longest time, it was just him and his mother—and they were *happy*. Up until when Henry came along. His mom remarried when Jason was only six years old. Henry never cared much for his new stepson. Henry thought the lack of a father figure had softened Jason up. Henry believed the boy needed to be *disciplined*. Taught *respect*. He made it his mission to turn Jason into *a proper young man*. Is this ringing a bell?"

Peashooter's mother didn't say anything. Only listened.

"The only thing you need to know about Jason is," Peashooter continued, "he loved to read. Whenever he was done with one novel, his mother always brought him another. Until Henry. Whenever Jason accidentally left his books out where Henry believed they didn't belong, Henry would punish him. But he wouldn't just beat him. Henry would let Jason choose his fate: 'Punishment A' or 'Punishment B.' Punishment A would be something like—*No books for a week*. While Punishment B was always Henry's fist. No reading or a black eye. The choice was always his."

His mother reached out for him again, but he pushed her hand away.

"Jason would rather be bruised black and blue than lose his books. But the more spirited Jason was, the angrier Henry got. So he'd only hit harder. *And harder.*"

Peashooter's mother was trembling. Her own eyes were wet now.

"Do you know what the worst part was?" Peashooter asked.

"What?" Her voice cracked.

"Jason's mom."

"What did she do?" The words were barely there.

"She didn't *do* anything," Peashooter snapped. "While Henry was *disciplining* Jason, his mom stood to the side and acted as if nothing was wrong."

His mother took hold of his arm. He tried to pull away, but she held on.

"I'm sorry, Jason. . . ."

"You don't get to say you're sorry!"

His mother refused to let go. "I'm so sorry for what I've done."

"You don't get to . . ."

Peashooter struggled against her grip. "You don't . . ."

"Forgive me."

"You . . ."

He fell against his mother and she wrapped her arms around him. The sobbing that seeped out from her shoulder wasn't of Peashooter, but of a boy, a little child, hurt and frightened. He pressed his face against her shoulder, burying it as deep into her coat as he could, the sound of his crying drifting into the amphitheater.

Camp Cannibal had fallen. The Tribe had disintegrated.

Time to go home.

*Now if I could just find my own mom and dad . . .*

All the kids had been reunited with their parents, except for me. I couldn't seem to find either of them anywhere. I felt my heart pound against my ribs as I watched the crowd thin.

*Where are they?*

They weren't waiting for me in the amphitheater.

They weren't waiting for me in the parking lot.

They weren't waiting for me in my cabin.

They weren't waiting for me in the main office.

I spotted a father who looked like he was on his own, his back facing me.

"There you are," I said as I rushed up and tapped him on the shoulder. "I was beginning to get worried you hadn't—"

The man turned around and regarded me with a puzzled expression.

He wasn't my father.

"Sorry, I thought . . ." I took a step back. "Thought you were my . . ."

"Have you seen my son?" The man asked. "I'm looking for Salvatore."

"Sal . . . ?" I should've recognized the resemblance. "You mean Capone?"

"Do you know where he is? I can't find him anywhere."

*The counselors! Somebody should probably let them out. . . .*

"Follow me." I took him to the brig.

Capone shuffled out into the bright sun, wincing like a mole. His father rushed up and pulled him away from the dazed counselors, a million and one questions instantly flooding out from his mouth—"Did you have anything to do with this? Is this your fault? What happened to your braces? Where's the administrator? Just what kind of summer camp do they think they're running here . . . ?"

George was the last to wander out from the cabin. Loose bits of his ponytail-free hair straggled in the wind. "Please tell me the nightmare's over. . . ."

"Looks that way," I said. "Most moms and dads made it up for Parents' Day. Can't seem to find mine, though. . . ."

"Pendleton, right . . . ? You're Spencer?"

"That's me."

George blinked, processing a distant scrap of information buried in the far recesses of his memory. "Your father phoned before this—this campers' coup d'état."

"What did he say?"

"He wanted us to know that he wouldn't be able to make it to Parents' Day."

My chest tightened. "Why . . . ?"

"Some last-minute business-related thing, I believe he mentioned. If we ran into any trouble, he suggested we try calling your mother."

*Lights fade on the Spotlight Dad's exit once again. Cue the strings.*

I took a step back.

"What about my mom?"

"We really didn't have much time to discuss it." George swallowed, his voice raspy. "But she seemed pretty insistent that it was your father's responsibility."

A tiny voice piped up in the rear of my brain, quietly

informing me what I already knew but refused to believe until that very moment. . . .

*Your parents aren't here, Spencer.*

They hadn't come for me.

*Neither of them.*

No matter how hard I tried not to listen, the voice grew louder.

*You're all alone.*

I looked over at Firefly's mom and dad struggling to understand how things had got to this point. He bowed his head, tears rinsing the ash away from his cheeks. They both clung to him.

"*How* could this happen?" they asked. "Is it something we did?"

It wasn't going to be easy to understand. But at least they were trying.

Nobody wanted to try and understand me.

Not anymore.

Peashooter had been right.

I found Sully in the crowd. Her feet hadn't touched the ground ever since her father first took her into his arms and lifted her up.

"I'm taking you to the hospital," I heard him say.

Sully shook her head. "But, Dad—"

"You're hurt," he insisted. "We have to get your shoulder looked at."

"Just one second."

Sully slid out from her father's grip and forced her way through the crowd. As soon as she saw me by myself, a look of relief washed over her face.

I didn't move.

We remained at opposite ends of the amphitheater, separated by everybody else's families.

Sully could sense something was wrong.

"What is it?" she mouthed from across the crowd.

I tried to answer, but my voice was gone. My lips moved without any sound.

Sully looked confused.

". . . *Elephant juice?*" she asked.

We held each other's stare for a moment before I broke away and faced the woods.

"Spencer?"

I heard the call of the wild, more luringly and compelling than ever before. And as never before, I was ready to obey.

Dad's off somewhere. Mom needs a break. They wouldn't miss me.

"Spencer—!"

A breeze blew through, swishing within the woods—and for a moment, the rustling leaves sounded like a thousand pom-poms bristling together at a pep rally.

The pines were towering cheerleaders swaying in the wind.

"Spencer—wait!" Sully tried one last time.

The trees cheered as I entered the woods.

*Go, Spencer, go! Go, Spencer, go!*

I heard them chanting all around me as I picked up the pace.

*Go, Spencer, go!*

I was sprinting now, faster with each footstep, the chanting growing louder and louder the deeper into the woods I went.

# Acknowledgments

Thanks to Kyle Jarrow, Chris Steib, Erik German, Isaac Butler, "Uncle" Rick Mullins, and Liz Deibel for braving those messy first and second drafts. To Rob Moor, Leiko Coyle, and everyone else who kindly shared their summer camp stories with me.

Eddie Gamarra deserves a parade in his honor. I am constantly striving to be the kind of writer an agent of his magnitude deserves. To Ellen Goldsmith-Vein and everyone at the Gotham Group, thank you for believing in me and these books.

Kevin Lewis never told me to hold back. He always told me to find the envelope, but instead of merely pushing it, he told me to rip it to pieces—and for that I am forever in his debt. Thank you for being the kind of editor writers only dream about. To Ricardo Mejias and everyone at Disney•Hyperion, thank you for putting up with me.

To Indrani, who gave birth to our son while I gave birth to

this book—you inspire me each and every day. Thank you for being there for me through everything.

And thanks to the amazing books that inspired this one—*Walden and Other Writings* by Henry David Thoreau, *Animal Farm* by George Orwell, *The Call of the Wild* and *White Fang* by Jack London, *Peter and Wendy* by J. M. Barrie, *The Merry Adventures of Robin Hood* by Howard Pyle, *Lord of the Flies* by William Golding, *The War Between the Pitiful Teachers and the Splendid Kids* by Stanley Kiesel, *The Boxcar Children* by Gertrude Chandler Warner, *The Butterfly Revolution* by William Butler, *Bless the Beasts & Children* by Glendon Swarthout, and *Children's Nature* by Leslie Paris.